Able Team charged hard up the ramp

The three warriors reached the top just as the terrorists reacted to the assault with a rush from the other direction. Two Ingrams and Lyons's Konzak exploded into action half a second before the enemy could bring their Kalashnikovs on line.

Then Quadra stepped into the middle of the hall with his arms outstretched. In each hand he held a flask of pink liquid.

"Go ahead and shoot," the terrorist leader shouted. "When one of these flasks hits the floor, the plague is released!"

Mack Bolan's

ABLE TEAM

ABLE TEAM
The World
War III Game

Dick Stivers

A GOLD EAGLE BOOK FROM
WORLDWIDE

TORONTO · NEW YORK · LONDON · PARIS
AMSTERDAM · STOCKHOLM · HAMBURG
ATHENS · MILAN · TOKYO · SYDNEY

First edition February 1986

ISBN 0-373-61222-2

Special thanks and acknowledgment to
Tom Arnett for his contributions to this work.

Printed in Canada

PROLOGUE

"The Americans think Project Hot Shot is their best-kept military secret. When you control that one missile, they'll have no choice. They'll give you what you demand."

Ignacio Quadra squinted at the speaker as if he'd just discovered an unrecognizable insect in his beer.

"Why do you tell this to me?"

The man who called himself Fred White smiled. The brooding, dark eyes told Quadra the smile was a lie.

"If it's that easy, what's to prevent us from doing it ourselves?"

"Unless you break the security codes on the site's computer, you won't convince the President you can use the weapon if cornered."

"I don't believe Russia has experts capable of breaking American computer security." As he spoke, Quadra locked eyes with White.

White grinned. "I have some unusual American geniuses who'll take care of that."

"More noncombatants to protect."

The KGB agent shook his fat head. "They won't be there. Our people will put the computer on the telephone line. The experts will work from elsewhere, maybe your base."

"That would be better. Where do we start?"

"By putting your people to work in the think tank. The Americans think of Puerto Ricans as nothing but servants.

Bid for and get their maintenance contract. They never notice the peasant who sweeps their floors.''

"What's the think tank got to do with the missile?''

"The plan for taking over the missile is one of the projections in the think-tank computer. To defeat the Americans, we use the Americans' own plan. A joke, no?'' White smiled the innocent smile of a cherub.

OLGA GILTCH, called "Glitch" by her hacker friends, looked up from her computer screen and said, "Hey, everybody, it's *Uncle* Fred." The slightly sarcastic emphasis on the word "uncle" indicated to her friends that she didn't accept Uncle Fred without reservations.

The other four looked up as Fred White entered the old stable that was their clubroom. Lovingly insulated and wired by James Giltch to give his daughter and her older friends a place to use their computers together, it was a snug shack with two walls lined with computer-height benches, chairs, a bookshelf made from raw lumber and even an old refrigerator that kept their soda pop cool.

Grinning, Fred White collapsed into an easy chair in the middle of the room. Despite the stuffing trying to escape the threadbare fabric, the chair was the most comfortable in the room.

Olga sighed and stored the program she was trying to write. She'd have liked to finish it, but White always demanded their full attention. She realized she'd still be using just a Commodore with a tape drive if it hadn't been for White. Her present IBM-PC with two disk drives and all the memory it could hold was a lot more exciting. Like the other computers in the clubroom, it had been a gift from Uncle Fred when he'd been particularly pleased with some information she'd found for him.

Olga turned on her wooden kitchen chair and waited for White to speak. Her blond hair was braided and pinned into a coil at the back of her head. Her blue eyes were wide and alert over a scattering of freckles. She looked like an average thirteen-year-old who had crushes on rock stars and handsome teachers. But her bedroom walls were decorated with magazine photos of the pioneers in computer hacking and she spent her spare time in the clubhouse, expressing her own computer genius.

Ursula Usher merely dimmed her monitor and turned on her old piano stool toward White. Ursula was the leader of the group by default because she was the eldest. At seventeen, she felt ancient and experienced compared to her fellow hackers. However, in this select group all that really mattered was what you could do with a computer. She felt she was among equals.

Ursula was seldom aware of her devastating effect on men. She was five feet nine inches of slender beauty, with long black hair and an olive complexion. Her black eyes seemed to absorb whomever she looked at. But she wouldn't have won a popularity poll at school. Her brains frightened off most of the boys, and those too stupid to know that brains mattered received no notice from Ursula. Relationships with girls were not much better. So few wanted to talk about computers most of the time.

Val Tredgett's fingers hammered at the keys. He was determined to finish the program he was writing before turning his attention to White.

Val had shoulder-length blond hair and cold blue eyes. He was tall for fifteen, but thin. As he worked, his profile showed a heavy stubborn jaw.

Finishing as much of his program as he felt he dared, he carefully stored the results on a disk before turning his attention to White.

Fourteen-year-old Manny Noris, short and plump, turned his chair away from the Kaypro he was using and waited patiently to see what White wanted. The pockets of his safari suit bulged with small tools useful to a tinker in electronics.

Zared Elvy—"Zorro" to his friends—couldn't quite tear himself away from the spreadsheet on the IBM-XT. He turned his doe-brown eyes on White, then jerked them back to the computer screen. Finally, sighing, he ignored the program and faced the visitor.

The KGB agent suppressed his growing impatience. To all appearances he was the essence of composure. He could afford to be. Before the day was out, these five brats would jump every time he spoke.

He looked at Ursula. Too bad she was so old, but she was a beauty nonetheless. Even Olga Giltch, now thirteen, was too old for Fred White's tastes, but perhaps when he had these kids tucked away where no one could find them, he'd honor her by taking her to bed. He wondered if another hairstyle would make her look younger.

When White finally had their attention, he said, "I have a surprise for you."

The five hackers waited silently.

"I've found where we might get extra hard disks and boards for the computers," he told the young computer geniuses. "There are questions of compatibility, and the place that's giving us these doesn't want to donate equipment that might be wasted."

He paused. No one spoke. He'd carefully prepared this fiction to guarantee the kids' cooperation. He was pleased to see it was working. He knew from previous experience that Olga's father would not be home for another hour. There was plenty of time.

White smiled. Then he continued, "I've arranged for a friend with a truck to take all of us to the warehouse. There'll be lots of room for your computers. You're to try the parts. Any that work for you you may keep."

"Why would your friend give away good equipment?" Zared Elvy asked.

White had expected the question and knew it would come from Zorro, the business genius of the group.

"He'll be there while you try things out. Nothing's packaged. When you're through he'll know what he has and if it works. You'll be doing him a favor, sorting all this unmarked stock."

White was relieved to hear the truck pull up outside.

"Hurry up. Let's not keep Yepes waiting. After all, he's been good enough to volunteer to drive us."

A flatbed with a canvas canopy stopped outside the stable. White played his trump card. He handed Olga a piece of paper.

"Run into the house and leave this note for your father. I'm sure we'll be back by suppertime, but just in case we're not, I want him to know where you are."

The sign of adult authority being communicated was sufficient reassurance for the excited hackers. They jumped to unplug their computers, while Olga ran to the house to place the note on the kitchen table.

"As we discussed..." it began.

Olga dashed back and unplugged her computer.

"Uh, Olga, do you think I might use the washroom?"

"Go ahead." She told him where to find it.

White entered the Giltch home. He retrieved the note, put it in the inside pocket of his rumpled suit and replaced it with a very different note. He stalled the time it would take to use the toilet, then returned to where the children waited in the back of the stolen truck. He smiled.

It was going to be a one-way trip, but their short lives would be useful, very useful. America would never be the same again, if it survived at all.

1

A hundred dwarfs assaulted Lao Ti's head with hammers. The naked bulb hanging over her cot divided in two, came together, divided in two again. She shut her eyes and tried to remember where she was. She couldn't.

Lao fixed on the first thing she could remember and concentrated on the dim past, gritting her teeth and refusing to acknowledge the pounding in her head. She hoped to bring her mind through time to her present surroundings—a filthy cell.

Her mind focused first on the face of Sensei Kemuri, her teacher of aikido for nearly twenty years. The sad Japanese eyes seemed to bore right into her.

She remembered him saying, "Choose carefully those you live with. Remember, you are also choosing those with whom you will die."

But she was alone. She wouldn't die with her chosen companions. From the time she'd first seen them in action, she had recognized in Able Team the type of people with whom it was a privilege to share both life and death. Whether she died now in this stinking cell or later in a battlefield with Able Team really made no difference. Either would be an anonymous death at the hands of terrorists, a noble death worth many lifetimes of uneventful, uncommitted existence.

She'd first seen Able Team in operation when terrorists had been trying to eliminate all the American computer scientists. Then Hal Brognola had offered her a chance to work with the Stony Man operation. She saw this as an opportunity to work with Able Team, eventually to join them. Although she was one of the world's foremost computer scientists, she gladly turned her back on that career to become an antiterrorist. It did not take long to discover that her understanding of computers was more vital than ever.

The change had meant less salary, no public acclaim and the certainty of anonymous death sooner or later. Whatever price she had to pay, it was worth it. Lao recognized in self-respect the ultimate virtue.

Trouble had been brewing in Washington on two fronts. Hal Brognola, director of Stony Man operations, had Able Team sent to stop ninja assassins who were terrorizing Washington. She'd been assigned to examine a computer in a high-security think tank.

The think tank used a Cray computer to do simulations of World War III. In these simulations the United States had been winning with greater and greater ease.

This think tank, the Susquehanna Institute, hired the best planners and thinkers to be found. These men and women of imagination spent their days dreaming up circumstances that could possibly lead to World War III. The computer system then applied known resources, troops and technical weapons to the scenario. Next the computer determined whether the United States would survive and whether the survivors could continue the process of civilization.

The results of these war games were given to General Hofstetter, whose chief occupation was keeping the President, the chiefs of staff and friendly powers informed of the free world's current prospects for survival. The positive results of recent projections had disturbed Hofstetter. Easy victories would inevitably lead to decreased defense budgets. He didn't believe the real thing would be nearly so painless.

It was time for the United States to start losing the majority of the World War III games. General Hofstetter had sent one of his programmers to the Susquehanna Institute for some clandestine alterations to the program.

The programmer—Lao remembered his name was Donald Knight—had gone to work at night, when no one was around with the authority to question him. Only the security and maintenance staffs worked the graveyard shift at Susquehanna. The thinkers and consultants relaxed elsewhere.

Knight had been allowed into the high-security area of the computer. The log book at the site showed he had arrived at 0030 hours, but there was no indication he had ever left. A thorough search uncovered neither the living Knight nor his body.

It's impossible to disappear from a high-security site. Yet Donald Knight had managed it.

General Hofstetter waited tensely to hear the results of the next war game. They were not the results he expected.

The simulation wouldn't carry through. The computer kept interrupting the program to fill every monitor screen in the institute with a large representation of the Liberty Bell. Hofstetter knew he could keep his secret no longer. He confessed his attempt to tamper to his old friend Hal Brognola and also told him about the missing programmer.

Lao smiled despite her throbbing head. It was easy to predict Hal's reaction. He'd investigate before reporting to the President. He wouldn't put his friend on the block until all the information was in. So Lao had been driven straight to the Susquehanna Institute to try to find out what was happening.

Lao was the only guest at the huge old mansion that stood all alone on the Susquehanna River. The security men made a point of staying out of her way, but the maintenance staff followed their routines as if the institute were in full swing, which it wasn't. Because the computer wasn't cooperating, the "thinkers" had been sent home and computer projections had been suspended. It took Lao several days to get the computer to function without filling the screen with the cracked bell. It took more probing of the computer's secrets to discover the thing Donald Knight had discovered— someone had added a patch to the World War III program.

The illicit new chunk of program introduced a bias for the United States. With the patch in place American planning would have to be extremely bad before the projection would show the United States losing.

Lao remembered shifting her chair out of the janitor's way, then leaning back to ponder her discovery. Someone wanted her adopted country to grow complacent, then lax. Who? It was apparent why Knight had disappeared, but how?

Lying on the cot in the strange cell, Lao winced as she remembered her own stupidity. Sensei Kemuri, her aikido instructor, had constantly warned her that concentration should not preclude awareness. She knew how to keep her subconscious sensors in place while she concentrated, but alone in the computer room, as she thought she was, she hadn't bothered.

As she pushed herself to her elbows, her brain exploded in a multitude of colors. She knew now that the janitor had blackjacked her. How could she have been so stupid?

She lay back on the cot, exhausted, content to have brought her memories up to date. She still had no idea how the cleaning staff had managed to remove her from the high-security site. Nor could she tell why they wanted her alive.

But she was too weak to care. She brushed some strands of shredded paper from her shirt, then drifted back into unconsciousness.

"DAMMIT!" Blancanales rasped. "Stop treating me like an invalid."

"Take it easy long enough to recover. Then I'll stop treating you like both an invalid and a fool," Myrna X. shot back at him.

Rosario Blancanales grinned. He loved the fire in the small nurse's green eyes.

"Lao Ti's missing," he explained. "And we're going to find her. As far as Carl, Hermann and I are concerned, she's part of the team."

The green eyes took on another type of fire. "Are you sure she's just team, Rosario?"

He shook his head—a gesture of helplessness. "There's no such thing as 'just team.' We put our lives in one another's hands every day. It's a special relationship."

"If you go running around now, you'll just weaken, have a relapse. That was a serious neck wound. I should know. I treated it."

Blancanales thought for a moment, then said, "Help me dress, woman. I've got work to do."

"I DON'T SEE all that high security Brognola was talking about," Gadgets Schwarz said. "I didn't think the National Security Agency was capable of this much subtlety."

Lyons snorted as he looked out the car window. "Enough grounds keepers and gardeners to keep the whole state. Did you see the binoculars flash in the dormer window? That's the snout of a Stoner staring at us out of those juniper bushes."

"I didn't catch the binoculars," Gadgets admitted as he stopped the car in a parking lot a hundred yards from the giant old plantation house.

Gadgets and Lyons emerged from the car and looked around. Blancanales and Myrna climbed from the back seat, Blancanales leaning heavily on a cane that doubled as a *jo*, or fighting stick.

"No road within a hundred yards of the house," Gadgets commented. "I'll bet they keep that lawn so soft no vehicle could get over it."

Lyons grunted. He was looking at the winding, concrete sidewalk leading up to the house.

It was a rambling, four-story affair. The oldest section seemed Victorian. Wings and extra rooms had been added at various times in its history. The extensive lawn was surrounded on three sides by the Susquehanna River. Boathouses on three sides of the property all had upstairs apartments, a good place to keep hidden watch on the river and far bank. The neat fields were bordered by stone walls and trees. Each field had been recently cleared and stubble filled some of the fields. Others were freshly plowed.

Lyons turned to Myrna. "You'll wait in the car. I didn't try getting you security clearance."

"Why?" Blancanales asked.

"She doesn't need the hassles."

Blancanales looked at Myrna and shrugged. Ironman was being considerate, but could never sound that way.

Myrna turned her back without saying anything.

The three warriors walked along the wide sidewalk to the front door. It opened before they could knock.

The doorway was filled by a big man in a brown suit. Everything about the man was large and brown. He stood about six feet tall and must have weighed enough to be a linebacker. His eyes were brown, as was his hair and his deep tan. The stripe in his school tie was predominantly the same color. His brown Brogans were crepe soled and the matching belt was heavy enough to use as a mover's strap.

"Yeah?" If a voice could have been brown, his would have fit the description.

Lyons didn't bother replying. He reached into the handkerchief pocket of his plaid sport jacket, produced an identification folder and handed it to the brown creature.

The man took it in his left hand and examined it.

"Presidential. What about the others?"

Gadgets produced a similar ID from his jeans jacket. Blancanales fished his out from the inside pocket of his neat, three-piece suit. Each ID was scrutinized carefully.

"The only time I saw another ID like these was when a programmer handed me one."

"Part of the team," Lyons told him. "We're here to see why she disappeared."

"Yeah? What agency you with?"

"You saw the signature on the identifications. Ask him," Lyons countered.

"The name's Petersen. I'm in charge of security here. How about you just answer my question?"

"I just did."

There was a moment's silence before Petersen sighed and stepped back out of the doorway.

He closed the door behind Able Team, then said, "You gentlemen are wearing. You can leave your weapons in my office until you're finished."

"Like hell," Lyons answered.

There was a pause—the quiet period just before a storm.

"We got rules here."

"Did Dr. Lao Ti check her weapon with you?" Gadgets asked innocently.

"You mean the programmer? Yeah, she did."

"Where is she now?" Ironman asked.

Petersen shrugged. "She checked in all right, but she never checked out again. She must have got out somehow. We really searched the place thoroughly."

"We'll keep our weapons," Lyons told him.

Petersen looked at the three grim faces and had a sudden inspiration. He wouldn't make an issue out of it. "I've made a complete report," he told them.

"Show us where she was working," Lyons told him.

Petersen shrugged and led the way along the hall and down a flight of stairs. As he walked ahead of the three stern, silent men, he seemed to feel the need to talk.

"She got the problem with the computer cleared up. We're back in operation, but there's no one but security and cleaning staff here right now. The institute is between projects."

"What was the project at the time the first programmer disappeared?" Blancanales asked.

"I'm not allowed to say."

"Shit! You want to talk to the President about it?"

Petersen shrugged. "This is a private institute working under government contract. I'd lose my job if I answered questions, even from the President. You'll have to get that information from the department that contracted our services."

Blancanales sighed. "Which department?"

"I'm not allowed—"

Suddenly Lyons had a big hand on the brown-striped tie. He was pulling the tie back and forth. Petersen moved with the tie as if he weighed no more than an empty shirt.

"Cut it out," the head of security blurted. His hand darted for his jacket pocket.

Lyons's free hand grabbed the gun hand and wrenched it upward. The jacket pocket tore and Petersen discovered he was pointing his own Charter Arms Bulldog at his own neck and could do nothing about it. His head still snapped back and forth as Lyons jerked the striped tie one way then the other.

"Let go of him and put your hands on your heads," someone ordered.

Three guards in gray uniforms covered Able Team with Uzis.

2

Blancanales had been the last one to emerge from the stair-well into the downstairs hall. An Uzi nudged him in the back. Two more guards approached from the other end of the hall. They stopped six feet from Ironman, who was obliging Petersen to hold his own gun against his neck.

Petersen was forced to open his hand and allow the Bull-dog to fall. It was either that or shoot himself in the neck from the pressure Lyons exerted on his hand.

Lyons let go of the tie and grabbed the heavy belt. One quick hoist and heave and the security chief flew into the barrels of the guards' Uzis. They stepped back for a clear shot, allowing Petersen to fall heavily to the floor, but their fighting reactions had not been constantly honed in battle as had Able Team's.

Blancanales's cane flicked behind him almost negli-gently. The tip caught the guard's right hand, pushing it to the side. He loosed a blast that tore a four-inch hole in the plaster wall. The tip of the *jo* stuck with the hand like glue, continuing to force it to one side. Blancanales's shiny black shoe introduced itself to the guard's crotch.

The guard forgot his Uzi and slumped slowly down the wall, both hands trying to smother the fire that consumed the family jewels. Blancanales bent down, retrieved the Uzi, then straightened and waited calmly.

Lyons moved in right behind Petersen's flying interference. Gadgets was a single pace behind him. Lyons's long leg lashed out. The sole of his combat boot smashed into the Uzi on his right, driving the barrel upward and the fixed stock into the guard's ribs. The guard flew backward, unable to recover his balance.

He came to an abrupt halt when his back smashed against the door at the end of the corridor. Lyons stayed right with him and plucked the Uzi from the stunned man's hands.

Keeping one hand on his weapon to prevent it from being lined up, Gadgets slammed his other fist into the side of the other guard's neck, temporarily paralyzing one side of the guard's body. The same hand chopped down on the guard's good wrist, freeing the Uzi. Then the electronics expert simply stepped back with the captured weapon, bringing it around to bear on the guard.

Petersen rolled to his hands and knees and did a rapid crawl between Lyons and Schwarz, scrambling to reach his revolver. Lyons, leaning against the door, wasted no time on the guard. Still holding the Uzi by the barrel, he took four long strides back the length of the hall, overtaking Petersen. Petersen was just reaching for his weapon when Lyons's combat boot smashed into the security man's ass, causing him to collapse on top of the .44.

"Just leave it there, Petersen. What's this about?"

Petersen looked around before moving. When he saw that all the weapons were in Able Team hands, he decided it would be unfriendly to make another try for his gun. He sat up slowly, making it obvious that he wasn't reaching for the Bulldog revolver. Lyons towered over him, glaring, waiting for an explanation.

Petersen licked his lips. "When a door is opened without the all-clear signal being given," he said, "the guards are instructed to move in on whoever entered."

"You examined our credentials, yet failed to give the all-clear signal." It wasn't a question; it was a judgment.

"You still had your weapons."

"Of course." There was contempt in Ironman's voice.

"We can't have that and maintain security." Petersen's tone was dogmatic, stubborn.

More security men poked Uzis around the corner from the stairs and through a door at the far end of the corridor.

"Tell them to go away before someone gets hurt," Lyons ordered.

"They won't listen to me as long as you're armed."

"Then they'll have to listen to me." Lyons raised his voice. "If you gentlemen in the stairwell and at the end of the hall can hear me, wiggle the barrels of your weapons."

The barrels moved. "I'm going to throw my credentials where you can retrieve them. When you've had a chance to check them, you can listen to what I have to say to your boss."

Lyons tossed his ID wallet with the presidential signature where a gun barrel could drag it inside the door without the guard showing himself.

"We'll stand around until you check that," Ironman said.

Four minutes later a voice spoke up from behind the door. "He has clearance right from the White House. I telephoned. No mistake."

Lyons turned to Petersen, who was still sitting on the hall floor. "You have this place sewn up tight? Your own men are the only ones allowed to carry weapons on the site?"

Petersen nodded.

"Two programmers disappear. You control who comes and goes. That makes you number-one suspect. You don't get my weapons."

There was angry murmuring from the stairwell and from behind the door, but no one could dispute Ironman's logic.

Lyons waited for his statement to sink in, then said, "Get up. We'll finish the tour—now."

Petersen stood up, leaving his revolver on the floor. Ironman scooped it, put on the safety and tucked the gun in his belt.

"Where was Dr. Lao Ti when she disappeared?" Blancanales asked.

Petersen pointed to a door. "The computer room."

"Let's go."

The gun barrels disappeared from the doorway at the other end of the hall and from the stairwell. A fourth guard, conspicuously unarmed, returned Lyons's credentials.

Reaching into his shirt pocket, Petersen produced a piece of plastic the size of a credit card. He inserted this into a slot beside the door, and the door slid open. Able Team and Petersen stepped through, letting the door slide shut behind them, cutting off the sight of the rueful faces of the disarmed guards.

Able Team found themselves in a room measuring twenty by fifty feet. A small desk near the door was bare except for a telephone. The room was dominated by a twenty-foot table and swivel-base conference chairs. The long wall on the left was made of triple-glazed glass from a height of three feet to the ceiling. A small booth in the middle of the wall gave way to a double door leading into the room containing the computers themselves. The only people in the office portion were two swarthy cleaners. One was using a vacuum on the hard twist carpeting; the other was dusting.

The wall opposite the glass held a huge paper shredder and a baler. A bale of shredded paper, four by four by six feet, secured by metal straps, was ready to be removed from the room.

"Hard copy doesn't leave this room," Petersen explained. "When a member of a project team is finished checking the hard copy, he puts it through the shredder. The regular conference room is upstairs, but it has only terminals and monitors. People need additional clearance to get at paper copy."

Lyons looked inside the computer room, which was dominated by the Cray computer. It resembled a pillar ringed by a bench, except the seat was four feet from the floor. Around it, grouped like servants, were four other large computers, all connected to the Cray. Four work stations with keyboards and monitors were clustered at one end of the room. Two large printers sat at the other end. Halogen outlets peeked from the ceiling like nozzles of an old-fashioned sprinkling system. The raised floor was covered with tiles, every fourth one of which was randomly dotted with half-inch holes. The tiles were dark green, the walls and ceiling a sterile white. Three swarthy cleaners were at work in the computer room.

"The Cray is so fast," Petersen explained, "that it can only talk to high-speed computers. The programs and data are fed to the attendant computers. They talk to the Cray."

"How do you get that out of here?" Lyons asked, nodding at the bale of shredded paper.

"The cleaning staff load it on a dolly and take it to the elevator. It goes outside and is wheeled to the parking lot. We don't allow vehicles closer than that."

"How come the entire cleaning staff is Puerto Rican?" Blancanales asked.

Petersen shrugged, indicating he thought the question trivial. "The company that bid on the cleaning contract hires them. They all have sufficient security clearance for the job."

"Too many Puerto Ricans," Blancanales muttered.

"You prejudiced or something?" Petersen's voice was surly, challenging.

"I ought to be," Blancanales said in a mild voice. "I'm Puerto Rican."

Lyons strode across the office and entered the computer room. The others followed. He walked slowly around the Cray, keeping his back to it. He completed the circle and began again. Then Lyons stopped and pointed.

"What's that?"

"That's a 650-02, the computer that receives the information from the Cray when it's finished its computation."

"Not that junk. The bell above it."

Petersen grinned at the level of Lyons's questions. "It's a telephone bell." The security man then launched into a lecture. "Telephone connections between computers are too easily intercepted. We have a rule for secure computers—no telephones or lines in the same room. So the bell rings in here, but the operator has to go into the office to answer the telephone."

"Shit!" Lyons answered.

He strode over to the 650-02. He wrapped his hands over the top and yanked. Nothing happened.

"Hey! Take it easy. That computer's worth a quarter mil," Petersen rasped.

Lyons ignored him. He braced a foot against the wall and tugged harder. The blocky cube of machine tilted forward, then crashed onto its face.

The silence that followed the crash was broken by a loud groan from Petersen.

Lyons stepped up on the fallen idol and looked at the wall behind it. He muttered to himself as Blancanales and Gadgets came over to look.

Gadgets let out a whistle. "How'd you figure that out?"

"Figure what out?" Petersen interrupted.

Gadgets turned to the security chief. "There's a modem on the back of the computer. It's connected to the telephone lines."

"Impossible," Petersen said as he moved over to take a look.

"The lines that ring a telephone are still telephone lines," Gadgets answered. "Only two wires run up to the bell, but all four come as far as the computer. A child could have hooked it up, but it would take some sophistication to match the modem to the computer."

Petersen looked at the wires and groaned again.

"We all have bad days," Gadgets told him. The electronics genius didn't mind sinking his barbs deep. Petersen had shown himself to be surly and incompetent from the moment he'd met them at the door.

Gadgets turned back to Lyons. "Give, Ironman. How'd you figure it?"

"I didn't. That Army programmer did. Left a message."

"What's the Liberty Bell that keeps showing up on the monitors got to do with it?" Petersen demanded.

Lyons looked blank. "'Liberty Bell'? I thought he meant someone had cracked Ma Bell." He turned back to Blancanales and Gadgets. "Let's go."

Blancanales and Gadgets looked at each other and shrugged. They tossed the confiscated Uzis into a corner of the computer room and followed Lyons.

Lyons didn't speak again until they were in the parking lot. Then he stuck his head in the window of the Stony Man car and asked Myrna, "Can you drive this thing?"

She nodded, then moved to the driver's seat.

He straightened and turned to Blancanales and Gadgets. "I want the cleaning staff followed. Brognola will arrange to have it done. In the meantime, keep an eye on things.

Myrna will be back with the car when we find me a taxi or rental car.''

"Why?" Blancanales asked.

"Paper shredders," Lyons answered as he climbed into the car. Myrna had pulled away and that was all the answer Blancanales received.

Myrna let Ironman off at a car-rental office on the outskirts of Harrisburg.

"Will you be at Stony Man?" she asked.

He shook his head. "I'll be seeing a general about a dog."

Myrna headed back to the institute, wondering whether she'd been given any information or not. Her preoccupation was broken when she didn't find Blancanales or Gadgets in the parking lot. She settled down to wait.

A movement caught the corner of her eye. Without turning her head, she looked in that direction. Someone in a guard uniform was approaching the car, keeping a bush between himself and Myrna. She strained her eyes, looking the other way without moving her head. At the edge of her vision someone else was approaching.

Myrna had no intention of being a heroine in distress. She put the accelerator to the floor and left tread on the parking lot. She'd let Stony Man find out what had happened to Blancanales and Gadgets.

3

General Alan Hofstetter had to admit he wasn't overly fond of civilians. They always felt they had a right to question military judgments, yet inevitably they knew shit-all about how those judgments were made.

The blond bastard who stood in front of Hofstetter's desk was almost as tall as the general's six-foot-three. He wore a plaid sports jacket, yellow shirt open at the neck and brown slacks. The only thing that kept the general from laughing in his visitor's face was the distinct impression that the visitor was every bit as tough and obnoxious as he was.

"Well, Mr. Lyons?" the general barked. "You used the name of an old friend to get you in here. What the hell do you want?"

If the civilian was intimidated by the unfriendly atmosphere, he certainly was good at hiding the fact. Uninvited, he pulled up a chair and sat down. If he'd delivered a formal document the declaration of war could not have been more apparent.

"How good a soldier was Knight?"

"Who?"

"The programmer you sent to tamper with the Susquehanna computer. Was he a skilled civilian in uniform, or did he know how to handle himself?"

The general stooped to neither evasions nor denials. "What business is it of yours?"

"My team has to clean up the mess you dragged Hal into. I can't do it without information. Give, or let Hal off the hook."

"I didn't hook Brognola. He hooked himself. I simply wanted him to get me into the President without having to explain my purpose to every secretary in the White House. He insisted on investigating before reporting."

"Terrific. You just called him an old friend. Of course, you had no idea that he'd do such a thing for a friend." Lyons's voice was colder than the hand of death. He sat motionless, waiting for Hofstetter to storm and bluster.

Instead Hofstetter leaned back in his chair and relaxed.

"You don't pull any punches, do you?"

"Pulled punches are energy wasted."

"Before I start baring my soul to a stranger, what makes you think you can clean up this mess?"

"It's a limited field. We've got a sixty-five percent chance of shaking something loose. We're good at shaking."

Hofstetter nodded. "I can see that. Donald Knight was a career man. Captured in Vietnam. Escaped. If he's alive, someone has his hands full. I tend to believe he was killed."

"What sort of projection was the think tank working on when Knight disappeared?"

"I don't know."

Lyons cocked an eyebrow.

"The brains that place hires think of themselves as creative. They come up with the scenarios. I get the reports when they're finished, but I never know their current project."

"Who would know?"

"The director of the institute, the so-called thinkers they had on that particular project and E-4."

"'E-4'?"

"You're not familiar with Ernest Cowley IV? I don't know whether to feel sorry for your ignorance of the centers of power or to congratulate you for having lived this long without encountering that particular pain in the ass.''

Lyons didn't prompt the general. He waited.

''E-4 has a computer for a brain, ice water for blood and garrote wires for nerves. He's the chief briefing officer for the CIA. As such, he knows just about everything that's happening. The Susquehanna Institute relies on E-4 to supply them with accurate information for their simulations. So he has to know what they're working on.

''Other than that, you're stuck with the members of the think tank. Frankly, I give you poor odds in that direction. Their contract with the government expressly gives them the right not to talk about a project until it's completed. They're mad as hell that I sent someone to tamper with their computer. To say they're intransigent is the understatement of the year.''

Lyons had gone to Hofstetter's office with a gutful of contempt for the man. He was surprised to find his attitude had changed.

Hofstetter was a man of strong beliefs and strong character. He'd bend any rules he felt necessary to achieve his ends, but would never dodge the responsibility or the consequences. Lyons found himself believing that Hofstetter had gone to Brognola to warn the President, not to extricate himself from the mess.

''Where do I find this E-4?''

''The farm. He almost never leaves it.''

The ''farm'' was the euphemism for the CIA training camp. At its rural setting near Norfolk, Virginia, the Central Intelligence Agency planned its machinations with the United States's political structure, trained its operatives and kept extensive dossiers on the power elite. The dossiers were all that had prevented Washington from disbanding the agency years ago.

"'Almost'?" Lyons asked.

"A fitness fanatic. Spends half his days training. The other half he crams himself with reports. Whatever he does, it works. Nobody knows what's going on half as well as he does. He does all his training at the farm—swimming, cycling, running, weight lifting. I guess he does have to be careful. The Russians would love to grab him. He knows everything about us worth knowing."

"'Almost'?" Lyons repeated.

"He's a triathlon nut. He competes in triathlons whenever possible."

"'Triathlons'?"

"Races in which the contestants must swim, bicycle and run. I'm told they're getting very popular."

"Sounds like fun."

"'Fun'? Imagine swimming two miles, cycling another twenty and then doing a marathon run. I keep fit, but triathlons are a painful way to kill yourself."

"Think I'll try one and see for myself," Lyons said. "Anything else you can give me?"

"Just two small pieces of advice. Stay away from triathlons and have Brognola get you presidential clearance before you approach E-4. He's a dedicated bureaucrat."

Lyons stood up. He didn't offer to shake hands. Neither did Hofstetter.

"Thanks." In the one word Lyons let Hofstetter know he appreciated the general's frankness.

"Pleased to talk to someone who can get to the point," Hofstetter replied, and he returned to the report he had been reading before Lyons had come in.

Ironman's next stop was the fortresslike concrete building on Pennsylvania Avenue that housed the FBI. A telephone call to the Justice Department across the street brought Lyons instant cooperation. Once across the moat, he was quickly shunted to the eleventh floor office of Simon Drew, the FBI's expert in computer crime.

"Glad to meet you, Mr. Lyons. Please make an appointment. I have to leave immediately. Helping out with a multiple kidnapping."

"Computers being kidnapped?"

"Often it would make more sense than kidnapping a company executive. Most companies would pay more for the return of their computer then for their CEO. But in this case, five young hackers have been abducted. I know the orders from Justice are to give you whatever you want, but I really must go."

Lyons seemed oblivious to Drew's impatience. "If you know they're hackers, you already have a record on them."

"Yes."

"What is it?"

Drew bit back an angry reply. He stood with one hand on the doorknob, anxious to leave.

"They're a special group, five of them, ages thirteen to seventeen, wizards at computing. They've even got their own company. We think they've been cracking the security on government computers."

"And they've all disappeared at once?"

Drew nodded.

"I'm coming with you."

The FBI man opened his mouth to object, but thought better of it. Justice had been explicit. "Grit your teeth and give him what he wants."

Drew nodded and led the way to the garage. Two other agents were already waiting in a tan Ford. When they saw the garishly dressed extra man, both raised their eyebrows at Simon Drew.

"He doesn't like it any more than you do," Lyons told them, "but I'm coming."

Drew just shrugged, his only comment on his helplessness to change the situation. He followed Lyons into the back seat. The driver took off with a screech of tires, more to express his anger than to show the need for haste.

"Tell me about these hackers," Lyons ordered.

"That I can do. I've met them, talked to them. That's why Smith—he's driving—and Yanofski wanted me along."

Smith spoke up. "What did you do, Drew? Flash your buzzer and tell them you suspected they were saboteurs?"

Simon Drew didn't seem offended by the question. "I posed as a customer. They run a thriving little business. Call it SIGNET. Computerese for Special Interest Group Network."

"What are they doing?" the other agent asked. "Selling illegal software copies?"

"Wish it were that simple. Among other things, they sell legal software copies."

"Legal copies?" Yanofski asked.

"That's what they are. Say you like Lotus 123, but you want it to do some other things, too. You bring them a copy of the manual and they write the program from scratch, put in the changes and additions you want, and a week later you have a souped up, legal copy. They don't touch the original program. They simply write a new one to do the same thing."

"What do they charge?"

"Plenty. They know the values of their service. They work through the mail. Most of the businesses that use them think they're dealing with an established consulting firm. One of the kids, named Elvy, is the business manager. He should be running American Motors. In two years they'd be bigger than GM."

"How do you know they don't keep copies of the popular programs and just modify them?" Smith asked.

"I ordered a couple of programs and compared them to the originals. They do everything the original does, but they're not written in the same way. I'd swear they were written from scratch."

"Why would this get them kidnapped?" Lyons asked.

"Beats me. Maybe one of the software companies wants some slave labor."

The joke fell flat.

"You said they were cracking security on government computers," Lyons prompted.

"I said that I thought they might be. I haven't a shred of proof. I know they could if they wanted to. After I bought the software, I tried to get them to break security on a computer. For a while it looked as if they'd go along. Then one day they froze, kept telling me it would be illegal and they wouldn't do anything illegal. I got the distinct impression they were laughing at me."

"That answers that," Lyons said.

The sudden silence in the car indicated that the three FBI men didn't see any answers.

"They took your identity out of your own computer."

Smith snickered, thinking Lyons had made a weak joke, but Drew frowned.

"That's exactly the way they acted," he admitted.

After a moment's silence Yanofski said, "We'll get descriptions and photographs from the parents. What can you give us now?"

"Not much. They'll have disks scattered all around their computers. They should give us some clue about what the whiz kids have been up to," Drew answered.

"Fat chance," Lyons muttered.

"That's what this work is, Mr. Lyons, sorting all the possibilities."

"Someone will have cleaned out the disks," Lyons said. Then he leaned back and stared out the window.

The three FBI agents exchanged glances and shrugs.

Smith took them north from Washington on Highway 270. Yanofski used the radio on a patch to the Maryland State Police.

After a quick and cryptic conversation he hung up the microphone and reported, "State Police are sure no one's in position to watch the Giltch farm. That's one good thing about the sticks—it's easy to spot someone else's surveillance." He turned to Lyons and explained, "The kidnapping note had the usual 'no police' clause, but the State Police are sure we can go right in."

They passed Rockville and turned in at a long lane leading to an old dairy farm. Following Drew's suggestion, Smith drove straight to the converted stable. James Giltch emerged from the house to meet them.

Giltch wore overalls, plaid shirt, heavy boots and a suitably battered, wide-brimmed hat, but he fit no one's concept of a typical American farmer. His blond hair fell to his collar and his full beard was neatly trimmed. He moved with an easy, loose-limbed grace that seemed to indicate that farming took little of his energy. His green eyes seemed better suited to looking inside people than to gazing at far horizons.

Giltch's first words were damning in their careful neutrality. "You're being too obvious, don't you think? Four men in a four-door sedan?"

Smith presented his identification as he answered, "The State Police have men all around. They've assured us no one's watching. There was little chance there would be, but it would have been nice."

Giltch nodded. "Yes, it would be nice to wrap my hands around one of the creatures who took the kids. I'd enjoy that. The kids were on my property. I feel responsible somehow.''

While he was talking, everyone climbed out of the car. By unspoken consent they went into the converted stable.

''Where are the computers?'' Drew asked.

Giltch shrugged. ''They disappeared when the kids were taken.''

''Not a floppy disk left in the place,'' Yanofski said.

The FBI men seemed to be taking turns casting speculative glances at Lyons, who had predicted there would be no disks. Lyons spun slowly on his heel, surveying the entire room.

''Files,'' he said.

''What?'' Drew asked.

''You said the kids ran a business. Where's the paperwork?''

''Come off it. They're only kids,'' Smith said.

Lyons ignored him and cocked an eyebrow at Giltch.

The farmer managed a weak smile. ''Zorro kept records of everything. His office is in the old hayloft, up those stairs.''

The investigators followed Giltch up a narrow set of unpainted steps to a low loft. The farmer turned on a light switch. In the middle of the floor, under the bare bulb, were an old desk, four wooden kitchen chairs and a four-drawer filing cabinet. The FBI men pounced on the filing cabinet like wolves on a kill. Lyons led Giltch to one side and talked with him, asking questions only when it was necessary to keep him talking.

Half an hour later Drew let out a low whistle. ''Did you know these kids took out insurance on their computers?''

Giltch seemed amused. ''What? On a couple of Commodores, an Atari and I don't know what else?''

Drew gave him an odd look. "Don't you know what they had?"

"Not really. I tried to keep only enough of an eye on them to make sure they weren't getting into mischief."

Smith rolled his eyes at that one.

"They're covered for seventy thou worth of equipment. That doesn't include disks and software." Drew paused and looked at Giltch. "They wouldn't think it fun to insure stuff they didn't have?"

"Did they pay the premium?" the farmer countered.

Drew shuffled the papers in the folder he held. "Yeah. Two percent—that was $140."

Giltch shook his head. "They wouldn't spend money for fun. Money always meant better equipment."

The FBI computer specialist continued scanning the folder. "Their valuations are low. If this list they did for the insurance company is right, they had very sophisticated equipment. It doesn't come any better without getting into large mainframes."

Giltch shook his head, too puzzled to speak.

"You're going to talk to the rest of the families?" Lyons asked Yanofski.

The agent nodded.

"I have to get back now."

"We can't take the time to drive you back."

"No problem," Lyons told him. He nodded to Giltch and left the loft.

Drew set down a folder and hurried after him. He didn't reach Lyons until they arrived at a pasture a quarter mile from the stable. Lyons leaned against the split-rail fence, talking into a small hand radio.

When Lyons had returned the communicator to a pouch on his belt, the FBI man said, "Give."

"I'm trying to find two programmers who disappeared from a high-security site. I know nothing about your case."

There was truth in those cold, blue eyes that locked on Drew's, but the FBI man was unwilling to drop his suspicions.

"How did you know the computer disks would be gone?"

"I know my enemy. They never take chances."

"Who's your enemy?"

"Who would dupe a bunch of kids into cracking the security on government computers?"

Drew sucked in his breath. "But the kidnap note..."

"A good way to keep everyone inactive, waiting for the ransom demand."

"Then you think the kids are already dead?"

"No."

"No?"

"The KGB would have no compunctions about leaving a bunch of gory bodies for the parents to bury. If I'm right, the kids are being put to work on something big. They won't be killed until either they fail or they succeed."

"Nice thought!"

"Isn't it."

Only then did Drew spot the hard, knotted muscles around Lyons's jaw. When he noticed that, the FBI man realized how close to the surface lay a torrent of repressed rage.

Drew steeled himself. The question had to be asked. "What now?"

"You do things your way, I'll do things mine. If I find a whiff of the children I'll tell you."

"We'll get you back to Washington somehow."

"I'm not going back to Washington." Lyons reached into his pocket and produced car keys. The tag held the name of a rental company. "See the car gets returned. I'm going to be busy."

"Where is it?"

"Your director's parking spot."

"It's not marked."

"Sure it is. No one else parks there."

Drew sighed. He didn't feel like arguing with the angry blond warrior. He didn't know why, but he trusted him.

The two men stood in silence until the throb of helicopter rotors filled the air and a Sikorsky jet started to land in the pasture. Then, without a word, Simon Drew returned to his partners, wondering if anyone could find the kids in time.

4

Blancanales and Gadgets had been waiting in the Susquehanna Institute parking lot for eleven minutes when the
Puerto Rican maintenance staff poured out of the rambling white building. Norman Petersen stood at a side door,
impassively checking them out while they shouted and
poured abuse on him.

Petersen showed no surprise when Gadgets appeared at
his elbow.

The security chief continued checking each worker from
a list containing a dozen names. As he worked, he ignored
the abuse and spoke to Gadgets.

"To save you asking, yes, it has something to do with
you. They're all quitting. Claim their contract said nothing
about working where people shoot bullets around."

"Give me your car," Gadgets answered.

"Huh?"

"Two of us are stranded until our car comes back. I want
to know where they go."

"I thought I was supposed to be the guilty party."

"There were only two sets of people in the building at
each disappearance—security and maintenance. Take your
choice."

"I'll drive. I want to see what happens."

"You can come. My partner'll drive."

For an answer, Petersen jabbed several times at a concealed button set into the doorframe. A uniformed guard appeared immediately.

"Yes, Mr. Petersen?"

"I'm leaving the building." Petersen handed the guard the clipboard. "Tell Janniki he's in charge."

"Yes, sir."

The guard closed the big door after them.

"We're not set up for this," Petersen complained as he led the way to a gray, four-door Buick.

"Any better ideas?"

The security man shook his head. Blancanales intercepted them as they reached the car. Petersen handed him the keys, then climbed into the back. Rather than leave both himself and Blancanales with their backs to Petersen, Gadgets also got into the back seat.

The Puerto Rican workers loaded themselves into three cars and headed south.

"Do they always arrive at work in so few cars?" Gadgets asked.

"What you got against car pools?" Petersen grumbled.

"You don't find twelve people in three cars a touch too efficient?"

"Lotsa room."

Gadgets gave up, but he suspected the Puerto Ricans had all set out from one location.

At Harrisburg the cars took neither 83 toward Baltimore nor 15 for Washington. Instead they chose 81, which ran through the Shenandoah Valley where Stony Man Farm was located. Before reaching the valley, the cavalcade turned west on Highway 70.

Blancanales worked hard at the wheel of the Buick. He dropped back as far as he could without losing sight of the three cars. It took considerable skill to keep them in sight without being too obvious.

"They're going to spot us sooner or later," he said.

Gadgets grinned as he pulled himself back into the seat. He'd been hanging out the window so the metal in the car body wouldn't interfere with his communicator.

"Hang loose. Stony Man is arranging reinforcements."

The three cars swung down a rutted side road leading toward the Potomac River. Blancanales pulled the Buick to the mouth of the road and stopped.

"We certainly can't go down this road without being detected," Blancanales said.

"It's too late to worry about that," Gadgets told him.

A dozen men brandishing assault rifles emerged from the bush. A semitrailer stopped right beside them.

"Hell!" Gadgets exclaimed. "I can't raise Stony Man with that chunk of metal in the way."

YAKOV KATZENELENBOGEN was the assignments officer at Stony Man when he wasn't leading Phoenix Force into battle in some remote corner of the suffering globe. He was waiting at the Stony Man helipad when the Air Force Sikorsky carrying Lyons set down. He signaled to the pilot to kill the engines.

Lyons peeled out under the still-turning rotors.

"Hi, Yakov. Where's Brognola?"

"Already headed to Washington to confirm your White House clearance with the CIA."

"He could use the telephone."

The one-handed Israeli veteran shook his head. "Politics. He phoned Cowley for the information you want. Cowley found six polite ways of telling him to go to hell. Brognola's getting you both clearance and additional ammunition. But wait a second."

Katz walked up to the pilot side of the helicopter and spoke to the pilot. "We have permission to hold on to you for a while. Check with your base, if you like. We'll refuel you. You'll find food, coffee and a bunk at the mess. It may be twelve hours or twelve minutes before we need you again."

"Yes, sir," the pilot snapped, and turned back to his postflight check.

Yakov walked Lyons back toward the main Stony Man building.

"Blancanales and Gadgets are missing," Katz said.

Lyons said nothing. Waiting for the details, he marched with his face straight ahead.

"Myrna didn't find them in the parking lot. She telephoned, then drove back here.

"Later, Gadgets reported in by radio. Right after you left the Susquehanna Institute, the entire cleaning staff walked out and loaded into three cars. Blancanales and Gadgets grabbed Petersen and his car and tried to follow them until we could find a full team to get out there. They last reported in just north of Hagerstown. Then radio silence."

Yakov waited for a response, but got none.

"I told the chopper to stand by. If we get word on Blancanales and Gadgets, you may want to go there. Otherwise we'll get you to Langley the moment Hal arranges your clearance."

"Thanks. I'll eat now."

Without another word, Lyons veered off and headed for the mess. He hadn't eaten since early morning and it was late afternoon. He didn't know when he'd have time to eat next.

Myrna found him attacking a twenty-ounce steak so rare the grain of the meat didn't show in the center. She sat down without being asked.

"Enjoying your meal?" Her voice was a chill north wind.

Lyons shoveled in a large mouthful and sat chewing slowly, thoroughly, not bothering to answer her.

"How can you sit there eating, when Rosario and Hermann are probably dead?"

He took a mouthful of baked potato and sour cream, continuing to ignore her.

"Pig! You sit there eating while they sacrifice themselves."

"Don't use that word!" Lyons's bellow startled the few people in the mess for early supper.

"Who else but a pig stuffs his face while his teammates are dying?"

"Call me what you like, but there will be no lives sacrificed while I lead Able Team."

"You can't keep them alive."

"I know that, but they are *not* sacrifices. Never say that again."

Myrna shook her head, trying to convince herself she'd heard correctly. "What are you talking about?"

"A sacrifice is something wasted. A choice sheep burned needlessly before some primitive god. There'll be no sacrifices here."

"But we always talk about lives sacrificed in war."

"Lies, except for Vietnam."

"What's this got to do with Rosario and Hermann?"

"Everything," Lyons told the small redhead. "The soldiers in a normal war are not sacrifices. They are people whose lives are carefully spent in service to their nations. In Vietnam we pulled out of the fight without preserving the principles we pretend to honor. Those lives were sacrificed, not by the generals but by the chicken-shit politicians who gave away the freedom of an entire nation to buy themselves a little peace at home.

"That will *not* happen with Able Team. We cannot deny the odds forever. Each of us will die sooner or later. But our lives will buy a bit of freedom from terrorism, a small respite from the law of the jungle. There'll be no sacrifices here! Each life counts."

Myrna was completely unprepared for the vehement speech from a man who usually considered it a waste of time to say more than two words at once. The deepness of his caring wrenched at her heart. She sat with her mouth open.

Lyons reached over and seized her hand, squeezing it until she had to steel herself not to wince.

"No talk of sacrifices," he told her, "and no more talk of death. Blancanales and Gadgets won't just lie down and die for anyone."

Then, leaving his steak half-eaten, he stood up so suddenly his chair overturned. He strode from the room.

FRED WHITE WAS EATING an early supper of borscht, black bread and liver sausage, all delivered from a nearby deli. He ate while staring across the arborite-and-chrome table at the five o'clock news.

There were no reports of the multiple kidnapping. He considered that a good sign. There had been nothing on the news about the disappearance of the programmers. He decided that when the police hadn't had any idea what to do, they'd suppressed the story. That was fine with him. They could tap Giltch's telephone and wait for the ransom demand. It would never come, but waiting for it would keep them inactive for another couple of days.

His reflections were interrupted by a gentle knock on the door of his efficiency apartment. He sighed, turned down the volume on the television and peeked out of the small viewing lens in the apartment door.

He'd never before seen the woman standing in the hall. The distorted, wide-angle view showed a woman who radiated force and self-confidence. The face, which was close to the lens, was finely boned. The crimson lipstick and jet black of the eyebrows were offset by subtle use of green eye shadow that focused attention on the clear green eyes. The woman wore a gray business suit, complemented by a red scarf and shoes. The fingers, which clasped a matching red handbag, sported long crimson fingernails, immaculately kept.

He opened the door as far as the safety chain allowed.

Before he could speak, the woman said, "Open the door quickly, Byli."

Byli meant "white" in Russian. From the peremptory tone of voice, Fred White knew he was meeting his mysterious controller for the first time. He quickly unhooked the safety chain and opened the door. Once inside, she waited for him to relock his door before walking over to the table. She turned off his television, then sat down opposite the half-eaten meal.

White realized that even without her high heels she'd be an inch taller than his five-foot-seven. Her voice was a husky contralto, much better controlled then her wobbly walk in the heels.

As he cautiously lowered his rounded form into the chair opposite her, she said, "Go on with your meal. But really, Byli, I'd have expected you to be better Americanized by now."

He gestured to the Russian food on the table. "Have some. Eastern European takeout deli. In Washington you just aren't up to date if you don't take home a deli meal twice a week."

She made no response to his pleasantry, but went directly to the point. "Your report of people making inquiries at the

Susquehanna Institute is most disturbing. We must move the project ahead more quickly. What results have you to report on breaking the security codes in the computer?''

"We are taking care of those investigators. Quadra's people walked off the job and two of the three who were snooping at the institute followed them. They followed them right into a trap."

"What results with the computer?" the woman insisted.

"It's too soon for results."

"Getting children to do the job is scatterbrained. I don't know why I let you go ahead with this."

"Because it works. They're the ones who rigged the Susquehanna computer for you to enable the United States to win easily. They're the ones who discovered the latest war game was based on taking over Project Hot Shot. Without them we'd have no plan."

"What good's a plan if we can't control the launch computer. Are those brats working now?"

"Not yet. We took the children to the base just this morning. Rivera is supervising setting up their computers. I intend to keep them neglected and frightened over night. It should make them glad to use their computers in the morning."

"Tomorrow is Sunday. How soon do you expect results?"

He shrugged. "You know these things aren't predictable. We will be able to coerce the children into breaking the code, but if we get them too upset, they'll be useless to us."

"What about the Army programmer Quadra had removed from the think tank?"

"He still resists. Oh, he does it cleverly. He pretends to work at breaking into the Project Hot Shot computers, but he never succeeds. We have been punishing each failure, but he seems determined to die, no matter how painfully."

"You've failed with him, then."

"We never expected success, but he had to be removed once he discovered our tampering with the Cray computer. We had him. It was worth a try."

"Now you've kidnapped another programmer from the same site, a woman?"

"That was in my report."

"Is she worth a try, too? We must crack the computer or we cannot launch the missile."

"It will be a black eye for the Americans when Quadra reveals just what they have hidden in that national forest."

"Fool! Do you think we go to all this trouble just to embarrass the Americans? When that missile explodes over New York City and people see the horror of it, the peace movement will dominate this country. It will be ripe for the picking. We did not smuggle our scientists into the country just to look at the technology, in spite of the lies you told that foolish Puerto Rican revolutionary. Quadra and his Free PR movement will take the blame when New York dies of a new plague sent in an atomic bomb from Washington. Make sure that happens, or you will die of much worse than that."

The woman paused long enough to let White digest the threat, then returned to her question. "Is the woman capable of cracking the security on the launch computer?"

"Judging by how quickly she uncovered the patches on the Cray, I'd say so."

"Then I'd say we have a good chance to put both her and the children to work. Use her maternal instincts. Use the American's stupid sentimentality about children."

"What have you in mind?"

"Do you not see it? Put the female and the children to work together. If you do not get results, torture one of the children. The woman might resist torture of herself, but as long as you're willing to inflict pain on the children, she'll do what you ask. To be safe, give them two days together before the torture starts. Give them a chance to become emotionally attached. Put on the pressure to hasten that attachment. Do you understand?''

"Of course.''

"Then do it. I am tired of my mole existence. If you deliver you will be well rewarded. If you don't, you will be dead.''

Having delivered her ultimatum, White's controller stood up, wobbled across the room and let herself out.

White sat looking at the closed door. A first-class bitch, but she knew her stuff. Yes, this Dr. Lao Ti person *would* crack the security code rather than watch children being tortured. She wouldn't know the consquences of her action until it was too late. It would be easy to have her believe they wanted only to expose the biological-warfare laboratory.

White leaned back in his chair and smiled his cherubic smile. Life would be good to him after New York was wiped from the face of the earth. Every country in the world would lose United Nations' delegates. Uncle Sam would find himself without a friend in the world.

5

Before Norman Petersen could react to being surrounded by armed men, Blancanales had rolled out of the driver's seat and under the tractor trailer that had stopped beside them. Gadgets had flung open the rear door and taken a long dive into the weeds on the other side of the car. Petersen had time only to huddle on the floor before bullets, searching for his body, annihilated all the windows.

Through the open car door, Petersen could see automatic rifle fire plucking at the weeds where the brown-haired warrior had dived for cover. The autofire struck ground farther and farther away as the gunners made sure they covered any distance their victim could have crawled or rolled.

Petersen pulled his Bulldog from his pocket. Suddenly the short-barreled .44-caliber five-shot seemed woefully inadequate. He clutched the gun and hugged the floor of the car, unable to raise his head far enough to find a target.

Petersen knew it was only a matter of seconds before the assault riflemen lowered their fire and shot him to bits, right through his Buick's thin body metal.

Then short bursts of extremely rapid autofire started streaking out from under the truck. One burst brought a scream as an attacker had his legs shot out from under him. The next silenced the scream. Then the cycle repeated itself.

The effectiveness of the white-haired fighter helped Petersen pull his own act together. He crawled toward the open door, looking for a target. A burst of bullets ripped into the seat beside his head. Instinctively he jerked back, but then he thrust forward to return fire when least expected. He was too late.

From the low dogwood shrubs that fringed the weedy area, a burst of autofire tore chunks out of the head of the gunman who'd shot at Petersen. The security man then knew that the brown-haired one had survived the heavy concentration of fire into the weeds.

One ambusher made the mistake of discounting the man in the car after so many bullets had torn through it. He exposed his back to Petersen to get a clear shot at Gadgets. Petersen lined up the small revolver and squeezed the trigger twice. Two .44s ripped through the killer's lungs. He went down coughing blood.

Emboldened by his success, Petersen crawled out of the back of the car. Only when he was totally exposed did he realize that enemy guns bore down on the car from fore and aft. The attackers had broken into two groups and retreated to where they were protected by rises of land from the shooting coming from under the semi. Both groups swung their assault rifles to bear on Petersen.

WHEN GADGETS HIT THE WEEDS he stopped short, huddling in a depression filled with fetid water. The fire brushed past him. Two bullets punched him in his flak jacket, leaving him unharmed. The heavy fire chased itself farther and farther from his position.

He was not dressed for heavy warfare, but he went nowhere without his Beretta 93-R and spare clips. He rolled over carefully and plucked the 9 mm automatic from its underarm harness. It was wet, but previous experience had taught him the sturdy gun was not hurt by a small amount of water. It wasn't fouled by mud; that's what counted.

Gadget crept slowly to a new position behind low, leafy shrubs. He could hear Blancanales's mini-Uzi raising hell from under the trailer that had blocked his radio transmission to Stony Man. Gadgets found a good fire position just in time to see Petersen crawl from the car right into the sights of a Puerto Rican nut who had been waiting for him to do just that.

Gadgets blew the goon's head apart with a 3-round burst of parabellums. In doing so, he showed his position to someone behind him. Even as he rolled Gadgets saw Petersen plug the gunman twice.

Crouching, Gadgets slammed home a fresh clip. At that moment, Petersen was an open target for both halves of the opposing force. He was dead unless Gadgets could pull fire from one side or the other.

Gadgets let out a bloodcurdling martial-arts *kai* shout and charged the closest group. Four Kalashnikovs jerked away from Petersen to zero in on Gadgets.

BLANCANALES LAY FULL OUT in a rut under the tractor, protected in two directions by the rig's wheels. He was thankful he'd switched from carrying a 93-R to the mini-Uzi. The rapid punch of the pistol-sized subgun was standing him in good stead. The fire selector was set on 3-round bursts, which tore out of the small subgun so rapidly he could visualize them flying in formation.

At first he did well, knocking out attackers' legs. When the killers toppled, he finished them off with head or heart shots. The survivors had hastily retreated behind two small rises of ground. He could no longer line up on their legs. By the same token, they had no clear shot at him. However, Blancanales wasn't fond of stalemates.

He rolled out from under the rig, keeping it between himself and the enemy. He crawled slowly around the tractor, ignoring the protests from his muscles. Just as he peered around a front wheel, he could hear the renewed bursts of gunfire. He gathered his legs under him, searching for enemy in the trees and shrubs.

When Blancanales heard Gadgets's fierce yell, he saw four Puerto Rican terrorists rise out of the bushes and bring the Kalashnikovs to bear on him. The mini-Uzi snarled in Blancanales's hands. A lightning figure eight of 9 mm bullets sprayed the killers, who crumpled to the ground.

Blancanales ripped the buttons from his shirt, yanking a fresh clip from a pocket in his flak jacket. His mud-stained vest was already buttonless. He ejected the old clip, slammed in the fresh one, then dropped the old clip to join two others in the side pocket of his jacket. There was a smear of grease from the clips, showing the path his hand usually took to the pocket. He continued to inch around the truck, searching for more trouble.

WHEN PETERSEN CRAWLED from the car to find two batches of guns bearing down on him, he was certain he was a dead man.

Then he heard a nerve-shattering scream and one group of guns swung to meet the more terrifying threat. Three assault rifles fired. The fourth merely dropped from the hands of its owner. He'd acquired two bullets in the heart and was no longer interested in assault rifles.

Petersen could swear he saw puffs of dust where a line of .223 tumblers stitched across the brown-haired warrior's abdomen. They didn't even slow him down. Although he didn't expect to live out the next three seconds, Petersen made a mental note to ask those two what brand of bulletproof vests they wore.

Three-round bursts knocked out two of the other three ambushers before they could line up their rifles. The last of the group made one pass, stitching bullets across Gadgets's abdomen. Before he could swing the rifle back, the barrel of the empty 93-R plunged into his eye, killing him instantly.

Gadgets dived, changing clips as he rolled over and over, but there was no fire from the other group of hardmen.

Petersen suddenly realized that he was not yet dead. Not even injured! He slowly turned to look at the other group of killers who had him sandwiched. They weren't there. Instead the white-haired warrior, the one Petersen was sure was under the truck, stood there, looking at four bodies as he fished a fresh magazine from somewhere under his shirt.

"Nice going," Gadgets told Blancanales.

"You didn't do so badly yourself, but you best check the end of your barrel before you fire your 93-R again."

Gadgets nodded, ejected the fresh clip, then the chambered round. Then he used a handkerchief and a twig to remove the gore from the end of the barrel. When he was satisfied, he reloaded and tucked the automatic back under his arm. He turned to Petersen.

"The surgeon general has asked me to tell you that crawling out of concealment into heavy cross fire could be hazardous to your health."

Petersen picked himself up. He knew he was grinning like a damn fool, but it felt so good just to be alive that he couldn't help himself. "Thanks," he said.

"Thanks yourself," Gadgets answered. He seemed preoccupied with a tangle of wreckage he'd removed from a small pouch on the front of his belt.

"What's that?" Petersen asked.

"Junk. Before it caught a couple of bullets it was a radio." Gadgets looked around to Blancanales. "Looks as if we find a telephone before we report to Stony Man."

"To hell with whoever," Petersen said. "We've got to tell the police."

Gadgets looked at Blancanales. "Should we tell the police?"

"Of course," Petersen interrupted.

"Who'll make the telephone call?" Blancanales asked. "The other two better mind the shop."

Gadgets caught the cue from his partner. "Someone else go. I'm too bushed."

"I'll go," Petersen volunteered.

Blancanales sat down on a small patch of grass. "Thanks," he told the security man.

Petersen hurried off in search of a telephone, looking back one last time at the lounging men. When he was out of sight, Blancanales and Gadgets started walking briskly in the other direction.

"STOP LOAFING. Get clean. You work now."

Lao Ti rose effortlessly from where she'd been sitting cross-legged on the floor of her cell. She examined the speaker carefully. She had not seen this Neanderthal giant before.

He was six-foot-four in his bare feet. The huge feet probably seldom found shoes large enough. He wore only jeans, supported by a wide belt, and a denim vest. His black hair was chopped within a quarter inch of his skull. He was clean-shaven, but this did little to relieve the impression of brute animal. When he grinned down at Lao he looked towering, unstoppable. His glistening teeth reminded her of the teeth in a pulp-mill crusher.

"You're better suited to crushing rocks," she told him.

He grinned even wider.

"Shower, clean clothes that way." He pointed.

Lao considered taking him. She wasn't sure she could. With little fat, he weighed twice as much as she did. She'd wait until she could catch him off guard. And she did need a shower.

She turned in the direction pointed and started to walk. Apparently it wasn't fast enough to suit the semihuman heap. A bare foot caught her on the ass and sent her reeling down the hall.

The shower room told Lao that her jail had once been a barracks building. The hulk slouched down on a bench where he could see into the shower room and gestured that she should go ahead.

"Where are the clean clothes?"

He grinned and pointed behind her. A man's blue work shirt and a small pair of jeans hung on a hook on the wall. She examined them. They were clean and about the right size. On the bench underneath were clean underpants and socks. She could do worse.

She ignored the huge male, undressed, showered, toweled herself and dressed. He watched, always grinning, but didn't try to molest her. She was almost sorry. If she could have gotten him preoccupied with sex, she was sure she could have killed him.

"Do I get fed?" she asked as she combed her hair with her fingers.

The big man looked at her speculatively before answering, "You get food soon."

Lao was herded down another hall and into a large room. To her surprise, the room held several computers and five suspicious young people. There was good light from overhead fluorescents, which was just as well, because the windows had been boarded over. The door locked behind her.

A blond-haired girl, who looked to be about thirteen, was the first to break the silence. "What do *you* want?" she demanded.

Lao looked around the room and over their suspicious faces. The only exits were the locked door and the boarded windows. She moved to the tables along the wall and looked at the computers. They were loaded with hardware: modems, hard disks, multifunction boards, special external ram-disk attachments, the works. Only after she'd absorbed the environment did she turn her attention to the five young curious faces.

"Other than wanting to escape, I want something to eat," Lao told the girl who'd asked the question.

"They haven't thought to feed us, either," said a boy with dark-brown hair, doe-brown eyes and wearing slacks, a golf shirt sporting an alligator symbol and Gucci loafers. He was by far the most neatly dressed of the teenagers.

"I'm Ti. What's your name?" Lao asked him.

"Don't answer questions," barked a shorter, younger boy. "She may be one of them."

The doe-eyed boy found himself looking levelly into Lao's eyes. In spite of his friend's warning he answered, "I'm Zared Elvy."

"We call him 'Zorro,'" said the eldest of the group, a stunning girl of about seventeen. Her black hair swung loose down her back. Her skin was smooth and tanned, and her eyes as black as Lao's. "I'm Ursula," the girl added.

Zorro grinned. "We call her 'U.U.' Those are her initials."

Once the ice was broken the others came forward hesitantly.

The one who'd warned Zorro not to speak identified himself as Manny Noris. Manny wore a safari suit; its pockets bulged with small tools.

The youngest of the five was the girl who'd spoken first to ask what Lao wanted. Her blond hair was braided and coiled at the back of her head. Her green eyes were direct, searching. She wore jeans and a T-shirt that promoted a rock group named the Orgasms.

"I'm Olga Giltch," she told Lao. "You can call me 'Glitch.' Everyone else does."

"I won't," Lao answered. "You're the farthest thing from a glitch I've met."

The answer won a smile and no argument.

The tallest was the last to be identified. He was a blond beanpole who couldn't have been more than fifteen. Already he stood five-foot-ten. He stared at Lao, his blue eyes remote, judgmental.

"That's Val," Ursula said. "He doesn't say much, but he's like a cross between a lion and a parrot."

Lao looked at the leader of the group quizzically, waiting for her to explain.

"When he talks, you'd better listen."

It seemed to be a standard joke with the group. Everyone except Lao and Val grinned. Lao acknowledged the introduction, such as it was, with a nod. She received a stiff nod in response.

"Do you know why we're here?" Lao asked.

Val, the tall blond, spoke for the first time. "So they can force us to betray our country," he said.

6

"Is this what you've been telling me?" Lao asked the young hackers. "You have your own company—SIGNET. Fred White hired you to check the security of various computers. He gave you telephone numbers and primary access codes and you were to see whether you could penetrate deeply enough to alter information or even to alter programming. You didn't know which computers you were penetrating."

"Usually we could guess after we got in," U.U. confessed. "He said we shouldn't know which people were his clients for security reasons."

"And he paid you in cash and by subsidizing the upgrading of your equipment?"

Nods from all five.

"When did you graduate from company computers to government security sites?"

Before anyone could answer the huge jailer returned, shoving a man in a rumpled Army uniform ahead of him. Then two guards wheeled in a dolly, holding trays of food and jugs of drink.

"Eat," the mammoth told them. "Soon work."

"I need to go to the bathroom," Glitch whined.

The big captor grinned. He pointed to a door beside the entrance.

"There. Private crapper. Real class."

The door closed behind him again, leaving the new captive with them. Lao and the five teenagers watched in silence as the soldier pulled himself together.

He must have barely made the height requirement. Lao guessed he'd be about five-foot-eight in his socks. He had red hair, a generous splash of freckles and more than a week's worth of red beard. As the door closed, he recovered from the last shove and slowly pulled himself erect. He looked befuddled, but Lao saw how quickly he sized up the room and its occupants.

"Tads," he breathed. "They put me in a room full of tads." The accent was Texan.

The remark brought a wry smile to Lao's face. She knew everyone had trouble guessing her age, and occidentals were often a long way off. She placed the soldier's age at twenty-four, about eight years younger than her. She made no effort to correct him, waiting to see what he would do.

The newcomer's gaze traveled to the cart of trays. "Food!" he exclaimed. "What are we waiting for?"

Everyone followed his lead to the food. They'd been well provisioned. The jugs contained coffee, juice and milk. Each tray held a steak and beans. There were mounds of buttered bread and a tray of fresh fruit. One thing aroused Lao's suspicion: cutlery was provided on each tray.

"Steak knives," the soldier said quietly. He sounded like a small boy on Christmas morning.

Everyone was ravenous. It took little time to dispose of the food. The soldier carefully wiped his steak knife and kept it in his hand when he slid his tray back onto the cart.

Lao made a point of having the others notice that she put her knife back, then waited to see what the youngsters would do. Val, the tall one with blond hair, started to follow the soldier's example.

"I wouldn't advise it," Lao told him.

Val looked at her suspiciously. "Why not?"

"It's too obvious. It's an excuse."

"Let the lad make up his own mind," the soldier drawled. "Sometimes a man's supposed to fight."

"A human always fights for freedom," Lao answered, "but the ones who survive don't walk into traps."

The redheaded soldier squinted at her. "How old are you, miss?"

"If you measure wisdom by the age of the lips that utter it, you're bound to a short life of folly," Lao answered.

"What's that supposed to mean?"

Manny Noris, the short boy in the safari suit, answered, "It means you should address the argument, not confuse issues by asking about the speaker."

Manny then returned his tray, putting his knife back with it. Val followed suit, then the rest of the young people. The soldier held his silence and scowled.

THE MAMMOTH JAILER ambled down the corridor to an office. Once inside he smiled at the man in the visitor's chair. Then he sat behind the desk. The expensive chair scarcely protested when he leaned back and put his bare feet on the desk. When he was comfortable, the big man, Yepes Rivera, reported to his dapper leader, Ignacio Quadra. His voice became soft, educated, like Quadra's.

"Well, Nach, all your actors are onstage awaiting your entry. I'm sorry I'll miss the show."

Quadra glanced at his Rolex. "The show has to wait until White shows up."

"Do you trust that jolly old bugger?"

"I trust him no farther away than I could screw a *señorita*. But the KGB are financing us and doing most of the planning, so we put up with him."

Rivera nodded. "You still got no idea who this mysterious controller is?"

"No, but I'd enjoy strangling the sarcastic bitch. She can't put together two words without a putdown."

"Let's face it, Nach, we've changed since university days. We'd both strangle someone just for the fun of it."

"What the hell are you talking about?"

"This thing about supplying those kids with steak knives just so you can go in there and beat the hell out of them. Is it really necessary?"

Quadra was smiling until the final question. Then his mouth tightened until his lips almost disappeared. "That's a stupid thing to ask. You know standard procedure for keeping prisoners compliant."

Rivera took a hunting knife with an eight-inch blade from a desk drawer. He started cleaning his fingernails with it, making Quadra wait for an answer to his question.

When he had his leader fuming, he said, "Sure, it's standard procedure. But is it standard terrorist procedure because it works or because we enjoy doing it?" He held up a hand to keep Quadra from interrupting. "That Oriental chick is something else. I watched her while she showered. But you know what I was thinking? I was wondering how much pain it would take to start her screaming."

Yepes Rivera continued, "When we were at Princeton, we were callow idealists. We were going to free Puerto Rico, whether it wanted to be freed or not. God knows, it needs freeing. They dump chemicals in our food until the boys are growing tits and the girls are reaching puberty at age three. So we formed Free Puerto Rico, or Free PR as we call it now, and started our acts of terrorism."

"That's the first step," Quadra explained. "You've got to provoke overreaction from the authorities to get the population on your side."

Rivera waved the knife back and forth, symbolically cutting off his leader's speech. "I know the cant better than you. I'm the one who went on to Patrice Lumumba while you stayed in the hills. Remember? I learned how to be a terrorist while you were bringing in the cash with the hijackings and bank jobs."

"And don't forget it."

"I won't," Rivera assured his leader. "But I'm making a point. I think we both realize we're not going to succeed. Even if we pull this deal off—stealing that Hot Shot missile—Puerto Ricans aren't going to want to give up their American connection. If our objective was all that mattered, we'd quit now. We keep going because we're addicted to causing pain and death."

Quadra stood up. "Yepes, old friend, your brains are fried. We do this because we must." He paused, then resumed, "I hear a car. That'll be White. I'll do my act now. Not because I like it, but because I have to. If you've lost faith, it doesn't matter. Because we're this far from victory." Quadra held his thumb and finger half an inch apart, then smiled at his old friend and left the office.

Rivera returned the knife to the drawer and shook his head. The bitch was right. Quadra couldn't react without deceiving himself. He sighed. He'd miss his friend, but that damn missile would be launched when the time came. And there would be no way to get Quadra to go along. He'd think he was selling out the cause. *¡Jíbaro valiente!* Why couldn't he see causes were for little people? What really mattered was power.

Rivera stood up, shook his head. It was time to transform himself into the animal once again.

LAO, KNIGHT AND THE FIVE MEMBERS OF SIGNET had lapsed into a period of lethargy, when the door opened. Fred

White entered, followed by six guards with Kalashnikovs at the ready. Last came a handsome, sharply dressed man who took charge of the proceedings. Lao watched intently.

"Good morning," the nattily dressed one began. "I'm Señor Quadra. I'm the one responsible for your being here."

Lao decided that Quadra believed what he said, but was incorrect. The sly smile on the fat one's face told her that he was the puppet master. KGB, she decided.

A guard had moved directly to the trays and checked the contents. *"Uno,"* the guard reported to Quadra.

The terrorist leader allowed his tanned, expressive face to show dismay. "It is terrible, is it not?" he complained. "We show you our best hospitality and someone tries to steal the cutlery. You must understand that I cannot permit such things to happen."

His eyes swept the room until they fell on the soldier, who still clutched the knife.

"Ah, Señor Knight, I see a steak knife in your hand. Perhaps you forgot to put it back?"

"Perhaps."

"If you'd be so kind as to put it back now?"

The redheaded soldier walked over to the cart and tossed the knife onto a tray. Two Kalashnikovs followed him each step of the way. The moment his hand let go of the knife, Quadra stepped behind him and slammed a fist into Knight's kidneys. Knight let out a gasp of pain, arched backward and dropped to the floor.

Quadra kicked him in the gut. When Knight doubled over, the terrorist drew back his shiny, pointed shoe to kick the soldier in the head.

"Don't be a fool," Lao said, her voice calm.

Quadra was so surprised by the quiet rebuke that he paused in midkick and looked at her.

"Give him a concussion and you may as well kill him," she told the terrorist in the same calm voice.

He put his foot back on the floor and turned to face her. "For a woman who arrived here in shredded paper, you seem to think you're indestructible. You really think you know why you're here?"

"You need us to break security on a computer."

"True, but I do not need all of you. Any one of you is quite expendable. That is the first thing you must remember."

Lao stood silently.

Quadra waited, seeming to relish the stillness. Then he whirled and kicked Val in the balls. The tall teenager fell to the floor, holding his crotch but not crying out.

"The other thing to remember," the terrorist leader said with a smile, "is that you are responsible for one another. The offender will not be the only one punished. Someone else will suffer even more. Think about it."

Quadra had finished his performance. He signaled the guards. One wheeled out the food trolley while two others moved close to their leader, escorting him out, rifles at the ready. The fat man and three guards remained.

Lao turned to Zared Elvy and Manny Noris. "Take Val into the washroom. Soak a towel in cold water and keep it on his crotch until he's feeling better."

They jumped to obey.

"I give the orders here," the fat man interrupted.

Lao turned to face him. "What do you want done differently?"

White wasn't phased by her aggressive stance.

"You ask my permission first."

"For everything?"

"For everything."

"Then may the boys take care of Val so you can have our full attention when you tell us what you want?"

"That sounds better. Go ahead."

The group sat in uneasy silence for ten minutes. Then the boys came out of the washroom. Val Tredgett was hobbling. His face was rigid, and he refused to acknowledge his discomfort.

When he had their attention, White told them, "You now know the rules. When you refuse to cooperate, you'll never know who will be punished. Tomorrow we'll have a new problem for you. You will have only twenty-four hours to break the security on the assigned computer and map out its program. The next day you'll be given a new program to feed to it. Is that clear?"

"We won't do it," Knight said.

White calmly slapped Glitch so hard she was knocked to the floor.

"Will you repeat that?" he asked Knight.

The Army programmer, his cheeks flaming red and his jaw clenched, shook his head.

"It's a pity you've suddenly grown so wise. The next time little Olga and I will give you all a fine display of love-making. Won't we, my little baggage?"

He reached out and squeezed her cheek. She spat at him. White calmly sank his fist in Lao's gut.

Lao saw it coming but did nothing to avoid the blow. Someone had to stop the chain of punishment.

White wiped the spittle off his grubby suit jacket. "Someone has a cool head," he told the group. "Pity. I could play this game all day. Get your equipment ready. I want no delays when we patch you through to the computer you must hack."

White left the room without escort. The three guards remained to watch the prisoners.

"We have to fight them, no matter what it costs," Knight exploded.

"You fight them," Lao told him contemptuously. She turned to the hackers. "Will you show me the systems you're using?"

THE HELICOPTER CIRCLED the training base known both as the "Farm" and "Camp Swampy." Most of the land was low and boggy, except in the direction of the ghost town. As he looked down through the helicopter's bubble, Lyons could see the small figures of trainees flitting from building to building in the ghost town, learning the procedure for clearing enemy from a built-up environment.

Lyons unstrapped his Colt Python and left it with the helicopter pilot. Ironman knew the CIA would disarm him the moment he stepped out of the chopper onto their precious farm. He'd rather trust the pilot with his gun.

As he emerged, running under the whirling blades, two young men in Marine uniforms met him, frisked him and loaded him into an Army jeep.

The Farm was a collection of ugly wooden buildings held together by too many coats of paint. The site was dominated by a red brick building that looked as if it had been borrowed from an English campus.

Lyons was escorted to the top floor of the main building. While the escort stayed in the hall, Lyons stepped into an office that looked like something out of the last century. Dark wood paneling dominated the room. One wall was lined with books. Even the huge desk was an antique.

The man who rose from behind the cluttered desk was no one's idea of the usual bureaucrat. He was a lean, hard six-foot-four. The sun had lightened his hair and darkened his skin until both resembled weathered oak. His three-piece suit shouted Ivy League, as did the heavy gold cuff links and the striped tie. He looked much more like the president of a sporting-goods conglomerate than a man who'd spent his life keeping up with the world's covert and dirty operations.

"Good afternoon, Mr. Lyons. What can I do for you, sir?"

Without a word Lyons placed his introduction, signed by the President, on Cowley's desk. Cowley spread it with one hand and read it with a single flick of his eyes. He didn't resume his seat, nor did he invite Lyons to sit down.

"What do you wish to know?"

"What scenarios has the Susquehanna Institute been working on lately?"

"That's privileged information."

"Fine. That document gives me the privilege."

"I didn't say 'secret.' I said 'privileged.'"

"So did I."

"You don't seem to understand, sir. The information belongs to the Susquehanna Institute. It's not mine to bandy about.' He gestured to the presidential message. "Not even the President has the right to demand that a private citizen reveal his secrets. Only a judicial order can do that." E-4 spoke as if he were enlightening a slightly retarded office boy.

"Lives depend on this."

"Lives depend on discretion, sir." There was no trace of spite in the way the word "sir" was used, but ample contempt showed in its frequent repetition.

"Then you refuse to give me the information?"

"'Refuse' is a strong word."

"What word would you choose?"

"I'm unable to cooperate."

"Your inability will be reported. If I lose members of my team, I'll talk to you again."

"Is that a threat?"

"'Threat' is a weak word," Lyons answered contemptuously. He reached for his document, but Cowley slammed his hand down on it, pinning it to the desk.

"You'll have to leave that with me until I have it checked. I suspect it's a forgery."

Lyons didn't bother answering. His right hand reached toward the document. As Cowley's eyes watched the hand moving right, Lyons's left hand flashed like a lightning strike, connecting a left hook to the side of the bureaucrat's head. Cowley staggered back, and Lyons calmly returned the paper to his jacket pocket and walked out.

The military escort drove him back to the helipad. When Lyons climbed into the chopper, he did something he could never explain, not even to himself. He pulled the handkerchief from his pocket, wiped his boot soles, then threw the hankie out onto the ground. As soon as he slammed the hatch the pilot took off.

Cowley stood at his office window and watched Lyons's departure. He pulled binoculars from his desk and saw the performance with the handkerchief. It meant nothing to him, and that bothered him. He put the binoculars back and picked up the telephone. He dialed an inside line.

"Yes?" The voice on the other end was feminine, seductive.

"You owe me a good night. He was a real bastard," Cowley told the woman.

"If you're up to it," she told him, and hung up.

Cowley lowered the handset into its cradle. He wondered why he felt both excited and soiled.

7

"I did what I was told," Myrna snapped at Lyons. "Now why the hell are you trying to get rid of me?"

"I'm not trying to get rid of you."

"Oh, no! First you tell me to move out of Stony Man. Now you're telling me to get out of my own apartment."

"What's this about?" Blancanales demanded.

Able Team and Myrna were sitting in the living room of a furnished apartment on Dupont Circle in Washington.

"She's wrong on both counts," Lyons answered. "I told her to rent a furnished apartment immediately. She's much safer at Stony Man and should stay there until we wrap this up."

The small redhead put her hands on her ample hips and glared at Lyons. "Why did you let me think I was being kicked out?"

Lyons was genuinely perplexed. "I didn't say that."

Blancanales groaned. "Ironman, when you going to learn that sometimes it takes more than one sentence to communicate? We were missing, you handed Myrna some money and told her to come to Washington and find a furnished apartment today. Right?"

Lyons nodded.

"You didn't say you wanted it for a base of operations away from Stony Man?"

Lyons shook his head.

"Of course she thought she was getting the boot from Stony Man. What else was she to think?"

"But I didn't tell her that," Lyons insisted.

Blancanales turned to Myrna. "You get the picture? You can't read between the lines with Ironman. There is no between the lines."

Myrna caught the picture. She turned to Lyons. "You telling me to go back to Stony Man?"

He nodded.

"Why?"

"I'm thinking of doing something you wouldn't want to be associated with."

"But you'll involve Rosario?"

"It's his choice."

"I want the same choice."

"You had her rent the apartment. She's involved," Gadgets pointed out.

"She deserves to make up her own mind," Blancanales added.

"I'll do it myself," Lyons said. He headed for the door.

"Hypocrite!" Myrna called after him.

He turned, puzzled.

"You pretend to fight for freedom to choose, but that freedom doesn't apply to your friends."

Lyons was silent. The others waited for his reaction.

He grinned. The remote, haughty face became warm when he grinned. "You only get freedoms you're willing to defend. You defend yours well. Your choice."

There was a sparkle in her green eyes when she told him, "Since I have a choice, I'll go back to Stony Man and pine. It'll be better if I can honestly say I don't know what you're up to."

She walked to the door, and Lyons let her out and shot the bolt behind her. Then he sat down on a coffee table facing the other two.

"I'm going to invade the Farm," he told them. "I don't want to risk involving the rest of Stony Man."

Blancanales grinned. "I've wanted to do that myself every time they foul up one of our assignments, but why now?"

"They're up to something. Guy named Cowley—they call him E-4—refused presidential orders to tell me what the think tank was working on when Ti vanished. Gave me a lecture on ethics, instead."

Gadgets exploded into laughter. "'Ethics'?" he choked. "The CIA? You sure you were in the right place, Ironman?"

"How does he expect to get away with that?" Blancanales wanted to know.

"If Hofstetter's right, because he's damn near irreplaceable. Cowley's trying to maintain that he thinks my authorization's a forgery."

"He can't get away with that."

"He can stall."

"So what do you intend to do?" Gadgets asked.

"Burglarize his office. It's all old-fashioned paneling. Knowing how the CIA loves steel safes, I'll bet there're two or three behind those panels."

"You think what we want will be in those safes?" Gadgets persisted.

Lyons shrugged. "Either that or something we can use for leverage."

"Blackmail the CIA?"

"We can't go through channels. They own too many people."

"So what have you in mind?" Blancanales asked.

Lyons got off the coffee table and sat on the floor. He pulled a sheath of papers from his pocket.

"Here's the layout," he began.

HALF A MILE from the apartment where Able Team was planning its raid on the CIA training site, the telephone rang in another furnished apartment. Ignacio Quadra answered it.

"¿*Sí?*"

"Are you ready?" The voice was sultry, sexy.

"For you? Anytime."

"You couldn't hack it, so just try to concentrate on your revolution."

Quadra hated the acid mockery in the voice. He sat silently, waiting for it to continue.

"Turn on your scrambler," the voice instructed.

He reached over and flipped the switch on the gray metal box beside the telephone. From this point on their conversation would be unintelligible to anyone tapping lines.

"Are you ready?" she asked again. The scrambler took the sultry tones out of her voice.

He sighed. "Everything is as you instructed. We have sixty hardened veterans. They are outfitted as campers and bird-watchers. We are ready to move when you give the word. Another twenty well-trained guerrillas will stay at our present site. They'll eliminate the captives and protect our backtrack."

"Are you counting the people you have cleaning the Susquehanna Institute?"

"No. We shouldn't need them. We thought it best if they remained there longer. They'll merely overbid when the contract comes up for renewal."

"It's a good thing you're not counting them. They're dead."

"What?"

"They were followed from the institute. They all walked off the job on some sort of pretext. They lured the men following them into an ambush. It didn't work."

"Who wiped them? I'll bomb the sons of bitches!"

"Take care of the most important things first. If they'd been picked up, you'd have had to eliminate them yourself."

Quadra bit his lip and said nothing. She was right, but that only made her more objectionable.

She paused, then said, "I'm giving the word."

"But the hackers haven't even started working on the computer."

"By tonight my inside person will have the modem installed on the computer that controls Project Hot Shot. He's already tapped a telephone line in another part of the building and brought the line to the computer, disguised as an electrical outlet. You must be in a position to move about the same time the access codes are broken. I've already dispatched six technicians to help you. They'll arrive at your camp at dawn. Be ready to move out then."

"Move where?"

"The technicians are bringing you detailed maps with suggested troop deployment on them. Project Hot Shot is hidden in the Spruce Knob National Recreation Area in West Virginia. The missile silo is disguised as a combination water tower and fire-lookout station. The facility that tends the missile is tunneled into the mountain underneath."

"So," Quadra breathed, "that's why it's so poorly guarded."

"They can only use guards who pose as forest rangers and tourists," the female voice confirmed. "You'll be able to take control of the underground complex quickly. Be careful in the laboratories. The germ cultures they're breeding aren't deadly, but they can make you pretty sick.''

"Aren't deadly? What's the point of germ warfare if the germs aren't deadly?''

Even through the scrambler, some amused contempt showed in the controller's voice. "This is the Americans' way of saying they don't deal in deadly germs. This flu bacteria is launched with a small nuclear device. It's designed to shoot the bacteria upward before the device explodes. The bacteria drift down through a layer of radiation and become transformed into something deadly. What is relatively safe to handle is equally deadly to the honest peoples of the world.''

"Cute.''

"This is why you require our technicians. They'll give you the proof of the way the missile works. You'll need that for the press conference you'll give from the site. Of course, you'll hold off calling the press until the Americans agree to allow Puerto Rico its independence. Then you can go home a hero.''

"Cut the shit," Quadra told his controller. "I know that the majority of my countrymen do not wish independence. They've been blinded by American materialism. But I do what's best for them.''

"That is the way a people's democracy always works," the controller agreed. "Now I have one other job for you.''

"Another job? Should we not concentrate on this?''

"It's connected. There's one man who can still cause trouble. He must go.''

Quadra sighed. The controller ordered these killings periodically. They were the price of Russian arms, like the Kalashnikovs that had all been smuggled into the United States in diplomatic pouches and in supply shipments. He never had enough information to know whether the killings were necessary to his Free PR movement.

"Who do you want offed?" he asked.

"This is what I want you to do. When the technicians arrive they will have a description of the man. His name is Carl Lyons.

"Leave only ten of your troops at the base. Surely ten brave Puerto Ricans can take care of two unarmed prisoners and five children. Give the other ten descriptions of this Carl Lyons and have them watch the CIA training base near Norfolk. Mr. Lyons will attack that base."

"Pardon?"

"Mr. Lyons will try to infiltrate the CIA base and steal information. That's my reading of the man."

"Then you know him?"

"I have been watching him and his team for some time. They're deadly. I met him only once. He thought I was an empty-headed party girl." The controller actually laughed. It wasn't a reassuring sound.

"What's this about a team?"

From the tone of the controller's voice when he asked, he knew she'd been waiting for the question.

"He might have two friends with him. They just happen to be the same two who shot up your cleaners."

"They'll die slowly."

"They'll die quickly or else they won't be doing the dying. Tell your men to let them enter the Farm. If they manage to leave alive, make sure they get no farther."

"And you want ten men to do just this?"

"If the CIA does not kill one or two, your ten men will not be enough. You had a dozen cleaners and they were in the ambush position."

"I find this difficult to credit, but I will do as you say."

"Of course you'll do as I say. You have no choice."

The line went dead.

Quadra cursed as he hung up the receiver. More changes in plan. And that bitch! She loved rubbing everyone's noses in her own shit. But she was right. He had no choice.

Of course, he hadn't revealed his full strength to her. He didn't trust her enough to do that. If these men were that dangerous, he would send twenty men. It wouldn't do to let anyone get away with killing members of Free PR.

His mind made up, he went to find a screwdriver to disconnect the scrambler. Quadra knew he wouldn't be returning to this apartment.

LAO PUSHED GLITCH GENTLY to one side and sat down at Glitch's computer.

"Have you tried speeding up your disk access this way?" Lao asked.

The Oriental's fingers blurred over the keyboard. On the screen the message read: "When the time comes, work on breaking the security codes. Don't be too efficient. We need time."

Olga Giltch reclaimed her seat at the computer and said, "I prefer a program like this."

She cleared the incriminating message from the screen and keyed in the beginning of a disk-speedup program, then typed, "Does Knight know about this?"

"I don't think that's a reliable way to do it," Lao answered. Then she moved on to the next hacker to spread her secret message of slow cooperation.

Knight, the Army programmer, intercepted her. "Are you telling them to cooperate with the enemy?" he demanded.

"Yes. Would you prefer to see them beaten?" Lao looked at him calmly, hoping intelligence would prevail. It would make no sense to expect head-on resistance from children.

"Traitor!"

Lao shrugged and turned to move on to the next computer. Knight made the mistake of grabbing her arm. She in turn grabbed his wrist and whirled. Knight found himself staggering across the room. He didn't regain his balance until he bumped into the wall. Lao sat down beside U.U. and began to talk computers as her fingers sent a different message across the screen.

Glitch passed them and said, "I'm going to show your disk-operating speedup to Zorro."

"Thank you, Olga."

Knight sat and scowled at Lao and the five hackers. When Lao had managed to convince them to try things her way, she went and sat near Knight. A guard repositioned himself to hear their conversation.

"Do you not think you should stop trying to exploit the young people?" she asked him.

"What do you mean?"

"You plan to resist, no matter how much suffering it causes them. That's exploitation."

"It doesn't matter. They're dead, anyway."

"Defeatist."

He looked at her, puzzled. They were interrupted by White, who came bustling in, his rumpled suit as grubby as ever. His breath smelled of garlic salami.

"Hook your computers to the telephone connections on the wall," the KGB agent commanded. "You have a permanent connection to the target computer."

When he saw the young people moving to obey, White turned to Lao and Knight. "What are you two doing?"

"Sitting," Lao told him.

He strode over and tried to slap her. She moved her face out of the way and his fingertips fanned past her nose.

"We don't have computers," Lao reminded him. "The members of SIGNET know what they're doing. Until they get started, there's nothing for us to do."

That Lao was right did nothing to cool White's temper. He tried to catch her with the back of his hand. Her hand flew up and he hit one of her knuckles, instead. The back of his hand hurt like hell. He grabbed it and glared at her. A terrorist guard snickered.

It was the tall, cold Val Tredgett who came to Lao's aid. He said, "Ti, could you help me. I'm stuck."

"Excuse me," Lao said in a conversational tone of voice. She rose and walked over to Val.

"What is it, Val?" she asked.

His screen told the story clearer than words ever could. The computer at the high-security site was never intended to be hooked up to the telephone lines. So the security was merely access codes based on the supposition that only people with a high security clearance would have access to the computer. Lao shuddered when she saw how easy it would be to take control of this computer.

"What about trying to gain access this way?" Lao asked. She leaned forward and began entering an instruction that was almost sure to trigger an alarm in the target computer.

Then something hit the back of her neck, stars exploded and she felt herself slipping into unconsciousness. She fought it, but the back of Val's chair seemed to rise and strike her on the chin. She blacked out, knowing she'd lost.

8

Able Team huddled in the thin light of dawn inside the shell of an old general store. The original, built-in counter ran along one wall. Behind that, gray shelves held only dust. The pine floor had once been dark red, but now only faint traces of paint were left between the cracks in the boards. From a small storeroom in the back, steep stairs led to the second floor and another set to the earthen basement. The back door had a new board at the hinges, testimony to the number of times it had been kicked in by CIA agents in training. None of the windows sported any trace of glass.

The three warriors did a final weapons check. Gadgets was carrying the usual Mac 10. The silenced 93-R rode under his fatigues. Blancanales carried his familiar M-16 with the M-203 slung under the barrel. His bandoliers held grenades offering only smoke or tear gas.

"It feels creepy to go into battle with rubber bullets," Blancanales said. "The other side doesn't know we're not shooting live ammo."

"They'll know soon enough," Lyons answered. He had left the Konzak behind, carrying a Colt Commando, instead. The Python rode his hip.

There were no secrets in the ghost town near the Farm, so the town wasn't heavily guarded. It had been a simple matter to penetrate that far. Now they waited quietly for the day's training exercise to begin.

The decision to use rubber bullets instead of blanks had been Lyons's. He felt their chances of merging into the urban-clearing exercises were poor. It would be better to pose as practical jokers with rubber bullets and allow themselves to be chased toward their target.

Each member of Able Team wore a cap and enough camou makeup to disguise his features. Hopefully, the recruits would think Command had planted them as a surprise part of the training and Command would think they were recruits on a lark. It was a thin gambit, but better than trying to penetrate the heavily guarded main building at night.

Two hours after dawn they heard a skirmish line of sentries moving through the deserted, ramshackle buildings, making sure they were free of children, reporters, transients and anyone else who wasn't supposed to be there. Able Team moved into the ancient, hand-dug basement. Each of the three warriors headed for a separate corner and threw a dark gray blanket over himself.

Three pairs of boots tramped the upstairs floor. Someone descended to the foot of the old stairs and shone a flashlight around. He hadn't waited for his eyes to become accustomed to the low light, so he failed to distinguish the mounds in the corners and their slight difference in texture from the mud floor. He went back upstairs and tramped out the door.

Able Team hung back five minutes before moving to the second floor, where they waited for the training exercises to begin.

Twenty minutes later the first team began to move down the dusty street. This group was called Green Team, and each trainee wore a band of green Velcro around his right arm. Two of them broke away and entered the old store.

Blancanales dragged the butt of his M-16 back and forth across the floor, slowly, mechanically.

"What's that?" a voice downstairs asked.

"Sounds like a branch. The MPs have just cleared the place," was the reply.

"I'll go look," the first volunteered.

Footsteps crossed the plank floor and creaked up the stairs. The moment the crew-cut head appeared above floor level, Lyons drew the back of his knife blade across the man's throat. "You're quiet or you're dead," he whispered to the trainee. "Get up here now."

The trainee continued up the stairs. As soon as he reached the top floor, Blancanales started down the steps, trying to walk exactly like the trainee.

Peering out the window, the other member of the Green Team didn't bother looking around. "No sign of Yellow Team yet," he reported.

Blancanales slipped a garrote over the man's head, but didn't bother tightening it. "You're dead," he said softly. "I'm taking your body upstairs. You'll have to wait until it's discovered."

The victim turned around while Blancanales was putting the garrote away. "Who the hell are you?" he demanded.

"Keep your voice down or do twenty miles with a pack," Blancanales commanded in him a cold voice. "Until you deadheads learn there's no such thing as a safe place, your survival chances are nil. I'm part of Transparent Team. Now move your ass. I don't have time to wait for your green brain to mature."

It was exactly the right weight of authority and contempt. The recruit had been listening to the same tone of voice for ten weeks. He obeyed with unquestioning desperation. No one looked forward to full-pack drill through the boggy paths of Camp Swampy.

When both trainees were upstairs, Lyons gestured toward a room at the back. "Go in there and close the door. Stay away from the window. You may smoke—don't use it for a signal. When a member of your team discovers your bodies, you're free to check in with the rest of the dead."

Lyons turned to Blancanales and Gadgets. "Let's see how many more think there's such a thing as a safe place."

Able Team went downstairs, leaving the recruits to keep out of sight. They had already planned their next move and waited patiently for the town-clearing exercise to begin.

Yellow Team swept the town according to the instruction manual while the instructors acted as game marshals. Each two members of Yellow Team had a marshal dogging their heels. Blancanales and Gadgets set mouths in grim lines. They hadn't counted on so many fully trained operatives. Lyons smiled.

Within minutes of the beginning of the exercise, eight members of Yellow Team had moved in to clear the building across from the old general store. In their excitement they had forgotten that a third of their strength should be covering their backs.

Lyons waited until the marshals were concentrating on the action. Four short bursts from the Colt Commando emptied a clip of rubber bullets and bruised the asses of all four marshals.

"You're all dead," Lyons shouted as he changed clips. The empty clip carefully went into a belt pouch. Able Team would leave no clues.

The three warriors burst out the back door not ten feet from another Yellow Team party. Gadgets fanned rubber bullets above their heads.

"Dead," he told them. "Transparent Team kills."

"Wrap it up," a marshal told the Yellow Team troops. "You were far too slow."

Another marshal noticed the lack of arm bands. "You're disqualified," he told Able Team. "Arm bands are required."

"I just told you. We're Transparent Team," Gadgets shouted.

Able Team took off down the back of the buildings, but hadn't made twenty feet before the marshals with the smarting asses charged into the alley.

"Stop those jokers," one of them yelled. "They're playing games with rubber bullets."

Lyons turned and sent a burst across the shins of every trainee and marshal in sight, causing howls of anguish and outrage.

There followed a chase such as the Farm had never seen before. Able Team ran toward the main building, pursued by a dozen of the training staff. The trainees followed, but were laughing too hard as they told one another what was happening. The trainees slowly dropped behind.

The Marine guards at the door to the main building weren't sure what to make of the entire scene. They glanced at one another in obvious puzzlement. Able Team reached the corner of the building and began to run across the front. Still recovering from his wounds, Blancanales was gasping for air but refusing to let up. Both Lyons and Gadgets had slowed down to keep pace with him. They were now running slower than the pursuit. At the last moment they veered and charged the Marines.

Their rifles were confiscated before the guards realized there was a problem. They were shoved toward the pursuers. Then the three men with camou makeup on their faces disappeared inside the building.

A blast of rubber bullets discouraged anyone from following Able Team through the doors

The furious instructors of Green Team waited thirty seconds before risking the doors again. By that time there was no sign of the three unidentified warriors. The Marine guards telephoned the officer of the day, who ordered the building surrounded.

Able Team spread out on the stairs. Blancanales proceeded slowly, waving Schwarz and Lyons ahead. Gadgets started to drop back to stay with Blancanales, but Lyons seized Gadgets's arm and dragged him along. The two warriors ran down the third floor corridor to Ernest Cowley's office.

Lyons tried the door. It was unlocked. He threw it open and stepped inside. Gadgets followed. They stood on each side of the door, weapons ready.

E-4 sat at his desk, calmly pointing a sawed-off shotgun at Lyons.

"I saw you coming," Cowley told them. "I assure you, this weapon doesn't take rubber bullets."

LAO RECOVERED CONSCIOUSNESS SLOWLY. She could tell from the kinks in her neck muscles that someone had tried to kill her with an axelike blow to the neck. But her attacker had struck too high and her neck muscles had prevented injury to the spine. She could hear the fans in the computers, but not much else. She opened her eyes to find a circle of faces around her: White, the guards, the hackers. Only the Army programmer, Knight, was missing.

"She's awake!" Glitch exclaimed. Their was relief in her voice.

Lao heard a groan and was surprised to discover it wasn't from herself. She sat up. The room spun and tilted. Her head throbbed. The bruised muscles on the back of her neck were cramping and going into spasms.

"You are all right?" White asked.

"Why?" Lao asked.

"Don't ask me," the KGB agent told her. "Ask Lieutenant Knight. He sprang from his chair and tried to kill you."

Lao managed to turn toward the groaning sound. It was too painful to turn her neck; she twisted at the waist, instead. Knight lay doubled up on the floor. Lao didn't have to ask what had happened. Knight had been severely beaten.

"Would someone rub my neck for me?" Lao asked. She had to stall until she could put her thoughts together. It would help if she could reduce the pain level.

"I'll send for some aspirin," White said.

"No drugs. Just my neck."

Val stepped forward and started to knead the cramping muscles.

"Harder," Lao ordered.

His strong fingers attacked the steel cables in her neck. It hurt like hell, but she forced herself to relax by telling herself every five seconds that she would endure only five seconds more of the agony. Three minutes later her head was clear.

She reached up and stopped the massaging fingers, giving them an extra squeeze of thanks. Val surprised her by putting his large hands under her arms and lifting her to her feet.

"See. She's all right," White said, his voice too hearty. "Now get back to your computers. It will go hard on all of you if you don't get control of that mainframe."

"Do it," Lao advised them.

She stood on her toes and gave Val a small peck on the cheek. Blushing, he led the way back to the computers.

Lao went over to Knight and knelt by him. White followed her.

"He tried to kill you," White warned her.

"He might yet be useful," Lao replied.

White shook his head, indicating he thought Lao was wrong, but did nothing to hamper her examination of the badly beaten man.

By Lao Ti's standards, no one could call himself a well-trained martial artist unless he could deal with the wounds and injuries acquired in training. Sensei Kemuri, her instructor, had insisted that each advanced student learn the arts of the traveling herbalists of China, who could tend to general health problems as well as set bones and treat injuries. So Knight received an examination from someone who knew more about dealing with severe beatings than would most physicians.

The Army programmer was conscious, but in too much pain to resist the examination. Lao rolled him onto his back and opened his shirt. One eye closed—the cut over it was still bleeding. Her fingers located two broken ribs. Knight's good eye opened wider when Lao opened his pants and slid them down around his legs. She could see he'd been struck in the crotch, probably several times. She could see no permanent damage.

"Tape for his ribs?" she asked White.

"Why?"

"He is no use to anyone like this. Either make him able to reach the computer screens or shoot him."

The KGB agent looked at her suspiciously. "Why are you being so cooperative?"

"I'm trying to keep the prisoners healthy until you make a mistake," Lao answered.

The fat KGB agent laughed and tugged at his baggy trousers. "All this and honesty, too."

He was still laughing when he indicated that a guard should bring her what she wanted.

Lao stayed kneeling beside the suffering Knight. The members of SIGNET poked at their computers, but it was obvious that their attention was much more on Lao and White than on their monitors.

When the guard returned with a first-aid kit, Lao expertly taped the ribs. Then she grabbed Knight under the arms and dragged him to the door of the washroom.

"Cold compresses on your balls until the pain subsides. You're on your own," she told him.

"Thanks for nothing," Knight said between clenched teeth.

"And thank you for your incompetence as a killer," she replied as she walked away from him.

He glared at her, but crawled into the washroom to follow her advice.

She walked over to the computers. The massage had relaxed her neck. Concentrating on Knight had helped her forget her own throbbing head. She wasn't entirely steady on her feet, but knew she had to keep going if she was to keep these teenagers alive.

White intercepted her.

"What were you about to do when Knight tried to kill you?" he demanded.

"'Do'?"

"You had your hands on one of the keyboards. What were you going to do?"

She stood in front of the round, bald man who was the same height as she was. She waved slightly as if she were adjusting to the deck of a boat in heavy swell.

"I don't remember."

"The hell you don't!"

She shrugged. "Does it matter?"

"I want an answer."

"I can't even make one up. I don't remember what I was doing when I was struck."

"What do you remember?" he asked. His voice dripped suspicion.

She blinked twice, then answered, "Val called me. I went over to look at his monitor. That's all, but we could ask him."

White gave a grunt of disgust. "How would he know what you had in mind? Go see if you can figure it out."

Lao meekly staggered over to Val's computer. The tall blond youth didn't look around. His screen was about the same as Lao remembered it just before Knight attacked her.

When she was behind him, his fingers typed, "How are you really?"

"You were a big help," she told him in a normal voice as he erased the question.

He started to make the entries that would foul their chances of getting into the computer undetected.

"I don't think that would be wise," Lao told him. "Have you done a search for an access code?"

The question caught Tredgett by surprise. It was a hopelessly inefficient way to solve the problem. The entire access code could be circumvented because they were already into the computer through the modem. The machine, with typical computer logic, would assume that since they already had access, they had the right access.

"But..." Val began.

"One step at a time. Mr. White is in a hurry, but it won't help to trigger rejection by the computer."

The nonsense communicated. Val said, "Okay. I'll find an access code."

Lao moved on to U.U.'s computer. The screen was filled with nonsense.

"I'm lost," the eldest member of SIGNET said.

"I'll try to help. Let me sit down for a minute."

Ursula Usher stood up and Lao took her chair. White came over to watch.

Lao set up an automatic program to bounce eight-letter combinations off the computer's recognition program.

"Why eight letters?" the KGB agent demanded.

Lao shrugged. "Programmers think in binary. Just a guess." She was wondering how much he understood. Things were getting sticky.

The computer kept feeding eight-letter combinations to the unkown computer. It was a tricky procedure. There would have been a program in place to recognize step one in the hackers's usual game of Vault Invaders and sound an alarm. Apparently whoever had set up the system had not considered any of the usual precautions against telephone interception. If the security was set up the same as at the Susquehanna Institute, the computer would never be allowed near a telephone line.

"Something is wrong here," White decided. "This is not the way these children did this before."

"I don't know how they did it before."

"Guards," White bellowed. "Make an example of this woman. She's stalling."

The watch station sitting atop a cylindrical water tank was exactly that: a watch station. However, those who used it were much more interested in watching tourists than in watching for fires in the Monongahela National Forest. If they did see a fire, they'd probably call the real forest rangers.

The water tank on which the watch station sat was not at all what it seemed. Towering above the pine and red spruce on a mountain slope overlooking Spruce Knob, the tank was nothing more than a hollow launch tube.

If the horn on the watch tower started to blare, the pseudorangers had sixty seconds to evacuate before the watch station blew into kindling to accommodate the launching of the missile from the mountain below.

The missile would climb almost straight up into the blackness of space. A short hop over the pole and fifty minutes later an atomic blast would light the skies over Gorky. And for the next forty-eight hours a horrible death would rain on Russia.

The three men in the watch tower were oblivious to the scents of pine and cedar that wafted through the ventilators of the watch station. They ignored the sweat that dampened their shirts. They hardly noticed the aches in their arms, tired from holding the huge binoculars they used to scan one group after another. There were more tourists than usual in the national forest that day.

"A lot of binoculars and telescopes down there," one observer commented.

"The Puerto Rican Bird-Watching Society," his chief answered. "They booked with the park office."

"Lotta gear for birders. Look at the size of that telescope the big guy's lugging. That's meant for watching stars, not birds."

The third man said, "Whatever they're watching, it must be on top of this friggin' tower."

"I don't like this," the chief said, reaching for the telephone. He never made it.

A piece of plastic was removed from the front of the tourist's "telescope." The men in the tower found themselves staring down the maw of a SAM-11 missile launcher.

Orange flame blasted from the back of the launch tube. Before the three men could lower their binoculars, the Russian-made surface-to-air missile burst through a glass wall of the lookout station and the entire doughnut-shaped structure disintegrated like kindling—as it was designed to do. Only one of the three watchers was alive to comprehend his 300-foot fall, but he was lucky—he broke his neck upon landing.

The parking lot for park personnel occupied the center of a heavily wooded area not open to the public. Its privacy kept taxpayers from wondering why the park required such a huge staff. Actually, every forest ranger, guide and maintenance person was an employee of the National Security Agency, paid to keep the location guarded without it appearing so.

Twenty of the staff were scientists and technicians who worked in rooms carved into the mountain. In the deep ultrasecret catacombs they maintained Project Hot Shot.

The missile was kept perpetually loaded with fresh batches of a flu virus that would turn deadly when they fell through a layer of radiation created by the atomic warhead carried on the same missile.

The computer that programmed the missile's on-board computer with its destination was kept updated and ready. Weather reports were fed into it every four hours.

Before the watch tower exploded, a large group of "bird-watchers," all male, all fit, explored the woods surrounding the parking lot. After the explosion they appeared in the lot from all directions and converged on the employee entrance to the main building. Binoculars and telescopes were strewn about the ground. Suddenly each birder sported a Makarov, a Kalashnikov and a belt of extra clips and grenades. Each also carried a gas mask.

Strangely, the employee door was steel, painted with a wood-grain finish. But it opened to gentle persuasion and four ounces of plastique.

Three cleanup personnel, who gathered litter around the park with sacks and pointed sticks, pulled Uzis from their sacks and took positions behind cars to shoot the first terrorists to move toward the blasted doors.

The most alert of the three managed to pin two attackers with his autofire. Then more "birders" came out of the trees and the three defenders died, cut down by volleys of 7.62 mm, 122-grain slugs.

A souvenir shop occupied the front of the building. There, a tourist family of two adults and two children had been studying packages of slides. A woman about sixty had been examining a book on botanical specimens found within the park. Three sales staff had been waiting patiently, content to let them browse.

Then four terrorists burst through the door, holding their Kalashnikovs high. The sales staff, whose secret mission was to guard the installation, hit the floor. Two were in a position to grab Uzis from their concealment under the counter. Just as they reached for them, the sound of the watch tower exploding shook the shop and caused the souvenir mugs to tinkle.

A grenade tossed over the counter neutralized two of the defenders before they could work the bolts on their weapons. The mother screamed and gathered her children to her. The book reader dropped to the floor as if she'd been knocked out.

The father whirled toward the door, temporarily too stunned to move. A short burst from a terrorist weapon sliced three slugs across the man's neck. He spun and collapsed, spurting the last of his life over his family.

The third clerk stayed low and inched toward the back room. As the attackers scanned the shop, looking for the last dangerous enemy, he rolled into the back room and hit a concealed panic button that alerted security. Then, armed with an Uzi, he crept to a desk. He expected reinforcements would cover the front. Then more would come through the door in the back room that led to the employee entrance.

One terrorist ran around a shelf and swung the butt of his assault rifle in the face of the cowering mother, smashing her jaw and knocking her sprawling. Then he bent down and grabbed the four-year-old boy by wrapping his hand around both his ankles. When he straightened with the boy dangling upside down, both mother and son let out howls of anguish. He quieted the mother by stomping on her stomach. She fainted.

"Surrender and we'll let the children go," he bellowed to the unseen clerk.

"Let the children go first," the NSA man called from the back room. He desperately hoped to stall until help arrived.

"You got three seconds," the terrorist answered.

"I'll surrender. Let them go."

"Your time's up," the terrorist shouted.

He swung the screaming child by the heels and smashed his head against the shop counter. There was the stomach-wrenching crack and then a silence broken only by the whimpering of the dead boy's eight-year-old sister and the whistling rasp of the mother straining to breathe with a rib puncturing her lung.

A smaller killer snatched up the terrified girl.

He yelled to the unseen defender, "She gets gang-banged if we don't see your hands in the air right now."

Concentrating heavily on the last armed man, the terrorists were neglecting the gray-haired woman who had been near the book rack and who had thrown herself to the floor. Verna Odger had been a WAVE in World War II and had not forgotten her training. She belly-crawled into the mess of human debris behind the counter. Blood soaked through her gray linen suit. She followed the reach of a dead arm until her hand closed about the grip of an Uzi.

It took her only seconds to find the safety and work the bolt. The snick was not loud and the terrorists were still focusing on the back room. The shorter man had grabbed the little girl and was laughing.

Verna peered around the counter and saw the terrorist holding his rifle in his left hand. His left forearm was under the girl's arms, pinning her to his chest. With his right hand he was tearing off her pants.

As the elderly woman readied the unfamiliar Uzi, the mother wrapped her arms around the terrorist's legs, trying to reach her daughter. The third terrorist dispassionately shot her in the head.

It was the terrorist's last act. Verna Odger aimed at his body and tried a short burst. She was unused to the weapon, so it spit out half a magazine before she managed to slack the trigger. The 9 mm avengers climbed up his arm, pierced the neck twice and found his brain.

The terrorist with the child dropped the girl in his frenzied attempt to bring his Kalashnikov to bear. That was a fatal error, for it removed Odger's unwillingness to fire. This time she kept the Uzi steady as she squeezed the trigger. Fourteen 115-grain maggots devoured his entire midsection.

The fourth terrorist ran around the counter and lined up on the prone woman's back. However, the NSA man in the back room used the distraction to advantage. He stepped into the doorway and neatly placed a 4-round burst into the back of the killer's head.

Verna Odger cradled the crying girl in her arms, saying soothing things, and walked behind the counter to hunt for ammunition for the exhausted Uzi. The compulsion grew from her firm belief that unloaded guns were dangerous.

The surviving NSA operative heard the door to the secure area open behind him. He turned, a grin of relief on his face. The reinforcements were too late, but better late than...

They were the wrong reinforcements.

The terrorist and the security man recognized each other immediately by their weapons. The six-foot killer, whose short hair was brushed forward, strongly resembled an overgrown Napoleon Bonaparte. He smiled as he calmly shut the door, but at the last moment tossed in an HE grenade. Bits of security man and hundreds of souvenirs glorifying the peacefulness of the national forest filled the shop with deadly shrapnel.

IGNACIO QUADRA MADE A GLORIOUS LEADER. Tall, handsome and not sly enough to pass responsibilities on to others while he took the credit, Quadra led the attack on the complex.

When his Free PR goons had gained control of the entrance to the secret missile site, it had been only too easy to toss a grenade into the souvenir shop. If the four sent to eliminate those in the shop had failed, the revolution didn't need them.

The two elevators serving the underground complex were blocked open so no one could use them. The terrorists didn't want to waste time looking for defenders caged in an elevator and didn't dare risk using them for attack in case the power was cut. They used the stairs, gunning down two unarmed employees who had chosen to walk between floors. As they descended, the walls of the stairwell changed from concrete to naked granite. At the bottom, the stairwell opened into a series of downward-sloping tunnels with damp, stone walls.

Quadra and thirty of his men moved cautiously but inexorably through the tunnels toward the heart of the complex. When they arrived in the working area, the naked wiring that ran along the roof of the tunnels disappeared behind accoustic tile. Bare rock turned into brightly painted metal panels. The rough-hewn floor was smoothed out with concrete.

The complex was much like the computer hidden in its bowels. Both depended on secrecy for protection. Too little thought had been put into defending them once they were under attack. Puke gas cleared out the first two work levels of the complex in twenty minutes. Armed defenders were retching too hopelessly to bring their weapons to bear on the gas-masked invaders. The NSA men died in their own vomit.

Twenty-one minutes after the attack began, the most secret missile base in the United States was in enemy hands.

When Quadra and his killers reached the bottom level, Quadra slung his gas mask around his neck and strode down the corridors while his armed goons tied up scientists and technicians.

Anyone who had no potential to supply information was separated from the others, herded into a carpeted office on the top work level. These unfortunates would be the first to be executed if the President of the United States balked at the terrorists' demands, so they were stored closest to the exits.

Two of Quadra's lieutenants trudged back up to the surface. One had been using a small radio to check with the lookouts and those wiping out the last vestiges of park staff. His radio messages brought a van to the parking lot. Eight Russian scientists and technicians climbed out and descended into the bowels of the complex. That four of the eight were young and exceptionally fit escaped Quadra's notice.

The other terrorist lieutenant freed the elevators for use, checked the placement of his guards, then walked to a pay telephone and put a call through to the White House. No call would be placed to the press yet. As long as the Americans thought there was hope of keeping their secret they'd cooperate.

10

When Lyons saw the shotgun in Cowley's hands he leapt. The gun roared, sending thirty steel balls toward Lyons's gut. The flak jacket and central trauma plate absorbed most of them. The three pieces of shot that penetrated the shredded jacket to one side of the plate had insufficient power to penetrate Ironman's abdomen.

Cowley's padded leather chair went over backward as Lyons smashed into him. As Lyons rolled to his feet and turned, Gadgets moved around the desk to cover Cowley from the other side. The CIA briefing officer found himself still in his chair, flat on his back, with unfriendly faces glaring at him from either side.

Simultaneously the third member of Able Team entered and said, "Marines are closing in fast," and the white telephone in Cowley's desk drawer, connecting him directly to the Oval Office, emitted a soft purr.

Gadgets vaulted back across the huge desk and ran to the office door. Plucking two smokes from his belt, he yanked the pins and let the spoons fly. Then he tossed them in each direction down the corridor. Seconds later both made a small whumping noise and filled the hall with green smoke.

Gadgets shouted into the corridor, "Don't take foolish risks. We're just here to talk to E-4. Those could have been the real thing."

From the way the coughing faded it seemed that the Marines were taking Gadgets's advice, at least long enough to regroup.

While Gadgets was giving the guards something to think about, Lyons dealt with the telephone. The drawer was locked, but the heel of Ironman's combat boot persuaded the front of the drawer to fall off.

He scooped up the handset and said, "Ernest can't come to the telephone. He's being punished for being a bad boy."

The voice on the line barked.

"Oh, it's you Mr. President. It's Carl Lyons. I'm trying to persuade Cowley that your order to cooperate is not a forgery. I wish you'd explain that to him." Lyons listened, then continued, "I'll tell you what your emergency is, Mr. President. Puerto Rican terrorists hold one of your top-secret weapons.... No, sir, I don't have information, but it's the only thing that makes sense. I need Ernest here to tell me exactly what the Susquehanna people were working on and a couple of other things. Tell him." The last statement sounded as much like an order as it did a request.

Lyons listened for a moment longer then said, "Yes, sir." He gave the handset to Cowley, who was still flat on his back. "It's for you."

E-4 and the President spoke for five minutes. Gadgets and Blancanales tensely watched the door. Before Cowley was finished, a telephone on top of his desk rang. Gadgets scooped that one up.

"Ernest Cowley IV's personal secretary and apple polisher."

As Cowley listened to the President from flat on his back, he scowled at Lyons. The CIA man kept saying, "I'll see what I can find out," or, "If you say so, sir."

The voice on the other telephone barked at Gadgets, "What do you guys want?"

"We just came for a briefing. We'll be leaving shortly."

"I suppose you want an airplane provided?"

"Nice of you to offer. We have our own transportation."

"Funny. Look, you must know by now that you can't get away with this. Why don't you surrender now. Maybe you'll get a lighter sentence."

On the other telephone Cowley's voice took on a note of confusion. "Are you *sure* you want me to do that? Surely he can wait until the emergency's over?"

Gadgets told the negotiator on the other telephone, "You're interrupting a business meeting," and hung up.

Cowley said a resigned, "Yes, sir," into the white handset, then passed it back to Lyons.

"May I get up?" E-4 asked.

Lyons shrugged. "Whatever you like."

As the humiliated Cowley struggled to his feet, he noticed the bloodstain on Lyons's shirt.

"You're bleeding," Cowley said.

Lyons wasn't interested in small talk. "Happens when I'm shot. The President told you to brief us?"

Cowley nodded.

"Don't waste our time."

Before Cowley could answer, the telephone on his desk rang again. He snatched it up and barked, "Yes?" He listened for ten seconds then interrupted, "This is Cowley. I'm fine. These gentlemen are here for a briefing. Send a doctor up, then leave us alone." He paused for a moment, sighed and said, "If you insist. This is code shit-cake."

He hung up and told Lyons, "The Marines won't bother us any more."

Lyons glared at him. Cowley added, "Code shit-cake means I'm speaking of my own free will."

"It fits," Lyons said, nodding.

Able Team and Cowley found chairs. A voice shouted down the hall, "This is the doctor. Don't shoot."

"Oh, come ahead. Everything's all right," Cowley shouted back. Impatience tinged his voice.

A burly doctor with a large medical bag cautiously peered around the doorway at the four men sitting around the desk. "Who's hurt?"

Cowley pointed at Lyons. "He took a full load of steel buck in the stomach."

"Hell! Have him call the undertaker. He looks able to do it."

"Couple shot got through my flak jacket. Seeing as you're here, you may as well disinfect the wound," Lyons told him.

"Certainly. Lie down on the desk, please."

As Cowley hastily cleared the desk, Lyons peeled his bandoliers, web belts, fatigues and bulletproof underwear. Then he stretched out on the desk.

Gadgets walked over and looked at the tattered flak jacket. "Hell, man. That was close," he breathed.

Lyons ignored him. "Get on with the briefing," he told Cowley.

"Now?"

"I'm leaving when the doc finishes. I expect to be filled in before I leave."

The doctor put his heavy case in the chair Lyons had vacated, opened it and extracted several instruments. He put a few to soak in a kidney dish of alcohol, then sprayed Lyons's wound with a local anesthetic that also acted as a sterilizer.

"The institute was working on a projection of what would happen if terrorists managed to seize our most potent weapons," Cowley began.

"What was seized today?" Lyons asked.

"Stop talking," the doctor complained. "You're using your stomach muscles."

"I'm not sure the doctor is cleared to hear this," Cowley said.

Lyons's hand shot out, grabbed Cowley's striped tie and pulled until the briefing officer's face was two inches away from his own.

"Are you telling me your own medical man isn't allowed to know about an installation that's occupied by terrorists? You want me to kill him so he can't read the papers tomorrow?"

He released the tie and Cowley collapsed back into his chair. Able Team was surprised to see the CIA man blush.

"I wasn't thinking."

"If you'd been thinking," Gadgets told him, "we might have been able to stop this operation. Now give."

Cowley leaned back and began to speak, and Able Team quickly realized why he was so highly valued by the administration. Without notes he was able to spiel off a short description of the secret weapon—the bacteria and the small, dirty nuclear device that would transform the germs into something deadlier than the black plague.

Cowley then described in detail the missile site and its security arrangements. When he finished twenty minutes later, Able Team could visualize the entire setup.

As Cowley talked, the medical man removed the steel balls and patched Ironman. Then the doctor rolled his patient over and gave him a couple of large injections in the hip. While Ironman reassembled his blasted clothing the best he could, the doctor quietly packed his bag and left.

"Why didn't you tell us this the first time?" Lyons demanded.

"This is the most sensitive secret our country has. I wouldn't share it with the President if I didn't have to."

"Cut the horseshit."

Cowley clamped his jaw tight. He wasn't about to admit that he stalled in order to gain sexual favors from another CIA department head.

Lyons changed tack suddenly, catching Cowley off guard. "Where is the terrorist base?"

"How...how would I know?"

"The same way you know other things. A Puerto Rican organization large enough to take the facility you describe doesn't exist without leaving traces. You'd have picked up those traces."

"Not this time."

Lyons moved like a striking cobra. He rose, grabbed Cowley by the tie and hauled him across the desk. When Cowley was lying belly down on the desk, Lyons accented his point by rapping his knuckle on Cowley's skull, one rap for each word he spoke. The first raps seemed playful, but they had a cumulative effect. By the time Lyons was finished speaking, it was all Cowley could do to keep from crying out.

"This horseshit stops now. Your agency is operating in this country. That's against the law. Tough! I get the rest of the story or the press gets to hear how you fouled up."

Cowley caught his breath. Neither he nor Lyons mentioned the real threat. The President was expecting Cowley right away. If Cowley was late, the President would know he was still not cooperating.

"This is something I only suspect. I have no hard information. If I do share my suspicions, do you three keep your mouths shut?"

It was the best ruse Cowley could come up with. If they said no, he'd be justified in keeping his mouth shut. If they agreed, they seemed like the kind of suckers who'd keep their word. This would prevent them from telling how badly the CIA had fouled up again. It didn't used to be like this. He spared a fleeting thought to wondering why lately the CIA botched up everything they touched.

"So the CIA is still tripping over its own mole. Why should we tell the President what he already knows?" Gadgets asked.

"'Mole'!" The word shocked E-4.

"Every time we cooperate with the Company, someone's waiting to bump us off. Of course you have a mole," Gadgets told him.

Cowley bit his lip. It was a nauseating thought, but it made sense. The silence was tighter than a drumhead by the time Cowley decided he had no choice but to empty the bag.

"There's a chance the terrorists stayed on CIA property," he admitted.

There were no exclamations of surprise or disgust, no changes in facial expression. The three warriors sat quietly and waited for Cowley to continue.

"We had...we have a training base not far from Spruce Knob where the Free PR struck. It was supposed to have been removed from the books. It wasn't. I found out by chance only yesterday."

"And you think you have no mole?" Lyons asked in a quiet voice.

Cowley clamped his mouth shut again. Dammit! He was a fool not to have seen the pattern before this. But he wouldn't give these hotshots the pleasure of hearing him admit it. He'd take care of the mole himself. Not only save the honor of the agency, but also put him a step closer to the directorship.

"Give us the layout of this nonabandoned site," Lyons ordered.

Cowley slid back a piece of paneling in the wall and opened a safe. He handed them a plan of the site. Able Team spread it on the desk and examined it.

"Shut up about this site," Lyons told Cowley. "If we're expected, you're the mole."

Cowley nodded. He hated to admit it, but that cold blond bastard made sense.

Able Team emerged from the building to be faced by forty grinning trainees and eighteen scowling instructors. Only the Marines managed to keep poker faces.

"Remember the motto of the civil service," Lyons yelled. "Keep Your Asses Covered."

Able Team jogged toward the ghost town and their van, which was parked beyond it. The recruits laughed and cheered. Four instructors had to be physically restrained by their cohorts.

Able Team moved through the empty town and started across a field.

Suddenly Gadgets yelled, "Gun barrels!" and threw himself flat, tripping both his mates.

Immediately the air was filled with the cackle of Kalashnikov's and the whine of angry 7.62 flesh-seekers.

11

Lao had enough. Of course she was stalling, but she was still recovering from being knocked out by Knight and was in no mood to accept another beating. She rose from the chair in front of Ursula's computer and stepped to where she'd have freedom of action.

One guard moved to the door and brought up his Kalashnikov to cover the entire room. Another guard, well out of the first's line of fire, stopped ten feet from Lao and kept his assault rifle on her. The third moved in, grinning, holding his assault rifle loosely, ready to use either the butt or the barrel.

"I object to this treatment," Lao said in a mild voice.

"Object all you want," the terrorist laughed as he jammed the barrel of the rifle at her stomach.

Lao's stomach moved to one side as smoothly as a matador escaping the horns of a bull. One hand closed around the rifle while the other grabbed the terrorist's ear. A hard tug on each added to the attacker's momentum, sending him whirling across the room. His fellow guards laughed to see the burly terrorist sent flying by such a small woman. Their laughter stoked the fire of the terrorist's anger.

He charged back across the room with a bellow of rage. Lao seemed to welcome the charge with open arms, but at the last moment slipped to one side. She grabbed two handfuls of shirt and spun the angry terrorist straight into White. The two collapsed in a tangle of limbs and rifle.

Lao looked directly at the terrorist covering her with his rifle.

"Are you going to shoot?" she asked. Her voice reflected curiosity, not fear.

The confused guard looked at White for instructions.

Before White could do more than curse the man with whom he was tangled, Ursula's computer beeped. The eldest hacker let out a small gasp.

The message on her screen read, "Access code recognized."

White picked himself up off the floor and moved to the computer before Lao could intercept him. She arrived one step behind him and read the message over his shoulder.

Swallowing her sense of defeat, Lao asked White in a sarcastic voice, "Do you still believe we're stalling?"

The humiliated guard pulled himself to his feet. Forgetting his rifle, he charged Lao. His hands were stretched out ahead of him. He wanted nothing more than to seize her and tear her into stew scraps.

Lao heard him and dropped into a crouch as she spun around. His outstretched hands flashed over her head. She straightened suddenly, her shoulder catching him in the pit of the stomach. The charging bull fell onto the table, rolled into Ursula's computer and sent it crashing to the floor.

"Fool!" White screamed. "Idiot! We had access through that computer." It was difficult to tell if he was yelling at the guard or Lao.

"You do have clumsy help," Lao sympathized, "but why fret? The same program can be set up on another computer." She pointed it out knowing that he'd have reached the same conclusion when he calmed down.

The frenzied terrorist rolled off the table into a fighting crouch. Lao kicked him in the face to help him straighten up, then turned back to White.

"Make up your mind," she told him. "Am I to help, or am I to be executed? You're wasting too much time."

The dazed, enraged guard, who had his own answer to that question, dived for his assault rifle. White stepped on the rifle, pinning the guard's fingers to the floor.

"Not yet," he told the guard. "If she stalls, you may have her. But it seems she can hasten our victory."

The guard yanked his fingers free and would have attacked again if the guard who was supposed to be covering Lao had not grabbed his arm.

There was an angry exchange in Spanish. Finally the beaten guard retrieved his Kalashnikov and retreated from the battle, shaking with anger and humiliation. The other two guards struggled to hide their laughter.

"You are not good at making friends," White told Lao.

"I stay alive," she answered.

"Not if I find you stalling. Set up the program again."

Lao went to do as she was told. She had to admit to herself that she'd run out of ways to stall.

ABLE TEAM WERE LYING in a field of clover on the edge of the CIA's training camp. The new crop was only twelve to fifteen inches high, not tall enough to hide in. The men separated as Death snapped his fingers over their heads. Their long weapons were filled with rubber bullets. The handguns held the real thing but were no match for assault rifles.

Lyons listened to the rattle of autofire from three sides of the field. "Kalashnikovs!" he yelled to Blancanales and Gadgets. He could tell the distinctive rattle of the weapons anywhere.

Blancanales and Gadgets both signaled that they had the message. Kalashnikovs meant they were not dealing with CIA types or Marine guards. They could kill—if they lived to have the opportunity.

"Smoke," Lyons yelled. "Gas around the van."

Staying low, Blancanales slid off his bandolier of grenades, checked the small breeze and used the M-203 to lay a barrage of smoke grenades along one side of the field, firing as quickly as he could reload.

"Take the flank," Lyons told Gadgets. "I'll provide the distraction."

Lyons crept to Blancanales and told him, "Hold position until you get an all clear."

"I'll help with the flank."

"No! You're too slow. You'll need your energy for a final sprint to the van."

Blancanales nodded, unable to speak. Lyons was right. His wounds had sapped too much from him and he'd not taken the time to recover. At the moment he was more liability than asset.

Lyons squeezed Blancanales's shoulder. It was as if he were reading his compatriot's mind. Then Ironman rolled away to keep them separate. Blancanales fought back his feeling of uselessness and finished his barrage of smoke grenades. Then he pulled off the bandolier of tear gas and quickly found the range to the van. He had little time because a wall of multicolored smoke was sweeping toward them from the side of the field.

Lyons leapt to his feet and charged the van just before the shroud of smoke reached him. When it engulfed him, he ran in a slow curve along the edge of the cloud. Counterfire searched the deeper smoke for him.

Gadgets waited until he was hidden by smoke before moving toward the side of the field. He curved back, hoping to come out at the end of the ambush line, not in the middle where he'd have to sweep his fire over a wide arc. As he ran, he drew his Beretta 93-R, thankful he had a few real bullets to use.

Gadgets burst from the smoke cover almost on top of a terrorist. He was kneeling so he could see over the weeds, squinting into the smoke, looking for traces of Able Team. The infiltration specialist had time only to turn his run into a leap and unleash a flying kick at the terrorist's head. The heel of his combat boot splintered the terrorist's skull just in front of his ear. Adding to the trauma, slivers of bone pierced the brain, causing instant death.

Gadgets didn't slow. He was in the open and didn't dare stop to confirm his kills. He ran across the field toward the van.

Three other ambushers trained their Russian-made rifles at the spot they'd last seen Able Team. A 3-round burst from the 93-R chewed through the skull of the closest. He died before realizing that the enemy was no longer in the area where he pointed his Kalashnikov.

The two others swung their rifles toward the charging threat. Gadgets veered back into the smoke and threw himself flat as 7.62 mm Russian peace envoys tore above his head. Then he crawled close to the smoke grenades, keeping his face deep in the clover where the air was still fresh so he wouldn't cough.

When he felt closest to the enemy, Gadget crawled out of the smoke. Scanning the edges of the smoke, the two terrorists apparently expected Gadgets to emerge farther. Instead the Stony Man warrior found himself within eight feet of one hell hound, who was so busy training his rifle in the direction he'd last seen Gadgets he was unaware that death lay at his feet.

The 93-R swung away from the easy target. Holding the fold-down front grip with his left hand, Gadgets carefully lined up on the terrorist who was twenty yards away. Three parabellums escaped from the warm Beretta in Gadgets's hand and tore into the killer's chest, two into the left lung, the third passing through the aorta. Dropping his rifle, the thug held his chest in a vain attempt to keep his soul from escaping through the three small holes.

The quick triple bark of the Beretta warned the other goon. He swung the rifle around, finger tightening on the trigger.

After he triggered the 3-round burst, Gadgets swung the barrel of the automatic and fired again, an instant before the terrorist. At eight feet he was not apt to miss, even on a shot that wasn't properly lined up. Two of the three parabellums smashed into the terrorist's shoulder, causing him to reel back and shoot far too high.

The next burst was more carefully placed. Three 115-grain judgments entered the terrorist's forehead in a grouping that could be covered with a quarter. They pronounced their death sentence before blowing a four-inch piece of skull from the corpse's head.

As the body began to fall, Gadgets headed for the van, slamming home a fresh clip as he ran.

LYONS HAD INTENDED to show just enough of his charge toward the van to keep the ambushers at that end of the field concentrating on him. However, the breeze briskly moved the smoke across the field. He was thankful Blancanales had used his entire supply of twenty smokies to cover the small field. It was barely enough at that.

Lyons had reached the side of the field, not the end where the van was parked, when he heard the tear-gas canisters exploding around the van and decided not to approach downwind.

He reached a corner of the field and doubled back up the side, his Python in his right hand. Running along, he had been able to keep his head clear of the smoke as long as there was some of it between him and the fighters around the van. But running down the far side of the field, he was immersed in it, and as prone to cough as anyone else. He could hear the ambushers coughing.

Lyons slowed to a trot.

A voice close by said, "Juan, hold your position."

Lyons swerved toward the voice and tripped on a terrorist smart enough to keep his face flat against the ground.

"Juan, you idiot!"

Famous last words. A .45 slug from Lyons's Python whispered death in the terrorist's ear.

Lyons trudged back across the field, zeroing in on the coughing, which came from a six-feet-four-inch terrorist whose mouth was wide open. Lyons dispatched a 250-grain, lead cough drop.

Another cough caused Lyons to veer toward the fence. A terrorist was facedown behind some weeds. His face was free of smoke, but there was suggestive coughing around him.

Farther along the fence a voice said in a hoarse whisper, "Raoul? Where are you?"

Lyons located Raoul as he spoke; he dropped to the ground and waited. With much stumbling and coughing, another terrorist climbed the split-rail fence and dropped beside Raoul.

"I heard shots. What's happening?"

"I've been doing some terrorist hunting," said Lyons, emerging behind them. "You're next unless you tell me where your base is."

The two Free PR goons rolled in different directions, trying to bring their Kalashnikovs up. They were far too slow. A .45 kissed each of them good-night.

Lyons listened for further activity on his side of the field. He heard none. He freshened the Python as he walked back toward the van.

GADGETS APPROACHED THE VAN so that the breeze blew the tear gas ahead of him. He heard the booming of Lyons's heavy-duty handpiece from the other side of the field. It would take Lyons a while to circle back and stay clear of the gas.

A small noise alerted Gadgets that someone was approaching from the direction of the van. He dropped to the ground. Close to his right, two quiet figures emerged from the tear gas and smoke, stopping to clear their eyes.

Gadgets raised his Beretta, but a noise from his left caused him to ease back to the ground. Two more terrorists had moved into the breeze to get clear of the gas. Gadgets, lying face down, was surrounded by armed terrorists.

BLANCANALES FINISHED FIRING his tear-gas grenades toward Able Team's van. They weren't terribly effective in the open, so he used all he had. Near his position the smoke was blindingly heavy.

Keeping his face in the clover where the air remained breathable, Blancanales belly-crawled toward the vehicle. It was slow, hard work, and his bruised body protested, but he refused to stop and leave all the fighting to Ironman and Gadgets.

THE FOUR TERRORISTS seemed to notice Gadgets simultaneously. Before he realized they'd seen him, four Kalashnikovs swung to bear on him. Gadgets, who was facedown, doubted he could move quickly enough to take even one with him.

"Well," one terrorist said in a low voice, "let's take him back to the camp and see what he can tell us."

"Not much use," said another. "They'll be killing the prisoners about the time we get there. We won't have time to question him."

"Which prisoners?" Gadgets asked. His tone was conversational and contained a trace of Spanish.

"All of 'em. The kids and the program—" The terrorist broke off, suddenly aware he wasn't answering one of his own group. He immediately triggered a burst at Gadgets.

Lyons's .45 boomed counterpoint to the fast natter of Blancanales's mini-Uzi. The terrorists wilted like ripe wheat in a hailstorm.

Ironman and Blancanales closed in on Gadgets as he picked himself up.

"You okay?" Lyons barked.

"A few slugs hit my shoulder," Gadgets reported. "The vest stopped them. I'll probably have a small bruise to match Blancanales's collection. I'm sure glad you got here before they went for head shots. You hear what they said?"

"Puerto Ricans again," Blancanales observed. "What's all this to do with Puerto Rican terror groups?"

Lyons's voice was grim. "Don't talk. Move! If Cowley's guess is right, we have a chance of getting to Lao and the kids on time."

"An *outside* chance," Blancanales said glumly as he climbed behind the wheel of the van.

12

Lao Ti sat down reluctantly at Manny Noris's Kaypro. The small Oriental tossed her hair and spread her strong fingers on the keyboard, booting the CPM micro to life. Once more she began to enter the program that would gain them access to a powerful government computer in some top-security site.

Lao still had no idea where the computer was or what it was programmed to do. She knew only that the effects of breaking into its command structure would be disastrous for her adopted country.

How long must she stall? She had no doubt Able Team would find her, but would they find her in time? She had been unconscious when taken from the Susquehanna Institute and still had no idea where she was being held. Knight was slumped in a chair about twenty feet behind her. Three guards with rifles watched everyone in the room. The slightest movement attracted their eyes. Lao could detect no slacking of their alertness.

If it were a matter of only her own life, Lao would simply attack and keep attacking until they were forced to kill her. Those tactics were useless here. Her actions could easily result in the murder of the young people by White or the guards. And if they weren't killed, any one of them could penetrate the ludicrous security on the target computer.

Fred White, the KGB agent, stood looking over her left shoulder. It was obvious he knew something about computers, but she couldn't tell how much.

Ursula, whose computer was broken, was beside Manny. Olga Giltch left her computer to confer first with Val and then with Zorro. After the quiet conversations the keyboards were rattled with renewed vigor.

Lao erred with some entry and had to correct it. When she started the program, it jammed and she had to debug it.

White struck her on the back of her head. She fell forward into the keyboard.

"You're stalling," he yelled.

Pain throbbed through Lao's head and neck. The blow had added to the effects of being knocked out earlier. She fought to keep a clear head and still pretend to be groggier than she really was—if it was possible to be groggier and still be conscious. When she was struck, Lao did have enough presence of mind to deliberately fall into the keyboard. The pressed keys added nonsense to the program.

She pulled herself erect in the chair. The room was tilting. She didn't have to fake her disorientation. She wasted no effort arguing with White. She simply cleared the screen and began again.

She worked slowly, checking each entry twice. She couldn't guarantee to keep her wits straight if her head was hit again.

White turned to Usher and Noris. "You understand what she's doing?"

They nodded.

"Is she doing it correctly?"

Again they both nodded.

"Keep a close eye on her. If the program fails, one of you dies."

Lao carefully completed the program and set it to run. The target computer rejected it.

"What did you do this time?" White demanded.

Lao shrugged, puzzled. But she didn't allow the problem to distract her from the problems of survival. As she shrugged, she collapsed to one side. White's fist whistled past her ear.

Lao let herself fall right out of the chair. When she hit the floor, she rolled and came unsteadily to her feet. She found the KGB man shaking with fury.

"Kill her," he screamed at the guards.

THE SITE, which Cowley claimed the CIA was supposed to have abandoned and didn't, wasn't far from where Blancanales and Gadgets had been ambushed. It was early evening before Able Team found the two barracks buildings and four large Quonset huts west of Hagerstown and not far from the Potomac River.

Once the van was parked, the three warriors carefully crawled to the brink of a hill that overlooked the site. They were dressed in gray combat fatigues and dark gray makeup that broke up the white expanses of their faces. Black watch caps covered Blancanales's and Lyons's heads. They were dressed for heavy combat and their bandoliers held no rubber bullets.

After ninety minutes of patient observation, they began detecting signs of life. As darkness began to fall, lights came on in one barracks.

"Now if we only knew whether we've found CIA or the Free PR camp," Blancanales muttered.

"That's Gadgets's job," Lyons answered. Then he told their penetration specialist, "Get in there and find out what we're up against."

Gadgets nodded and faded into the dusk on the hillside.

Lyons then told Blancanales, "Get the van into position for sudden evacuation. Monitor the communicators."

Blancanales knew he was being shunted to a less active role, but didn't argue. He had to accept his teammates' judgment that he wasn't fit for combat. He slipped down from the hill, then trudged back to the van.

Lyons moved slowly, cautiously, across the site, a shadow among shadows. He moved as stealthily as Gadgets, but it took him much longer to cover the same ground. Ironman and Blancanales were experts at infiltration, but no match for Gadgets.

Lights came from only one building. Whoever was occupying the buildings was making no attempt to hide his presence. Gadgets decided to check out the other buildings first. The lit one would be the most difficult to penetrate.

The darkened barracks was boarded up. Gadgets flitted from window to window, checking each hoarding to make sure it was secure. All the doors were padlocked on the outside. No one would be staging a counterattack from that direction.

The first Quonset building was dark and locked. However, the door was held with a spring lock, not a hasp and padlock. From the small tool kit he carried, Gadgets pulled a thin strip of spring metal and used it to slip the lock. Inside, the place looked like an office: desks, chairs, empty file cabinets. But all paperwork had been removed.

Gadgets let himself out. A slight grunt as someone put all his might into a blow was all the warning he had. He threw himself flat as a rifle butt whistled over his head.

Gadgets rolled, kicking the shadowy figure. The force of the missed swing plus the combat boot to the back of the knee toppled the assailant. Gadgets wondered if he had a legitimate guard, or had he found the terrorist base.

The shadowy gun-swinger fell on his back. Gadgets rolled on top of him and pressed his right forearm heavily across the Adam's apple while his left hand closed around the rifle. He made no attempt to grab the weapon but simply kept it at bay as his hand slid along its length. He felt a four-groove banana clip and the distinctive wood grip behind the barrel. A Kalashnikov! No further questions.

The terrorist slipped his rifle past Gadgets's questing hand and tried to swing the barrel at his head. Gadgets ducked, increasing the weight on his forearm. The swing glanced off one shoulder. Gadgets smashed his left fist into the terrorist's armpit and his arm went limp. However, Gadgets did not let the pressure off the neck until the throbbing in the jugular stopped.

Gadgets rose to his feet and looked around, fighting to control his heavy breathing. He could see no indication that the fight had attracted attention. He bent down again and searched the corpse in the starlight, unsure of what he would find.

The contents of the pockets gave the owner away by their simplicity. There was a pack of cigarettes and a book of matches. A Makarov rode under the terrorist's left arm. The only money was one bill—Gadgets couldn't see the denomination. There was no change to rattle and nothing that would act as personal identification, not even a key. A spare clip for the Russian-made automatic was in one pocket and spare magazines for the Kalashnikov were in pouches on the belt. Nothing else. This terrorist was stripped down, ready for a raid.

Gadgets dragged the body inside the office. When he left, he let the latch click shut.

The next two Quonsets were padlocked, sealed tight. The last one was unlocked. Gadgets pushed the door open and threw himself to one side. Nothing happened. He crept in and shut the door. When the latch clicked shut, the lights came on. Apparently they were wired to go off when the door was open to prevent light from spilling into the night.

The building was being used as a garage. Three cars and a four-ton truck with canvas over the back were parked inside. Four startled terrorists looked up at Gadgets from their interrupted card game. Then they each dived in a different direction to recover their Kalashnikovs.

"DON'T SHOOT HER!" Olga Giltch shouted. "It's not her fault she couldn't get into the computer. We already used the code. We're in now."

Lao saw a sudden light dawn behind White's eyes and shuddered. White had been threatening the young people to force Lao and Knight to cooperate. Only now was it occurring to him that things worked even better the other way. The naive and inexperienced hackers would work to break into the computer if they thought that by doing so they could save Lao's life.

Lao contemplated forcing the guards to kill her. It would waste so few seconds that he decided against it. She'd stay calm and look for a better chance. What were the chances she could smash all the computers before she was killed? She decided the odds were next to zero. She had to stand stoically and play the cards as they were dealt, stay alert for some kind of a break.

White signaled for the guards to disregard his order to kill Lao. He pointed to a chair beside Knight. "Sit there. We'll see if these children can perform well enough to save your life."

Lao shrugged, glided to the chair and sat down.

"You were trying to stall?" Knight whispered. He sounded as if he believed White had made a mistake.

Lao ignored him.

"Thanks for the first aid," he said in a more normal voice.

"You're welcome." Her tone did not invite further conversation.

"Why didn't you tell me what you were doing?"

If he kept talking this way, he'd get them both shot now instead of later. Lao reflected that "later" wasn't that far off, anyway. The hackers were working like mad, ingratiating themselves with White, trying to save Lao's life. It would do little good to point out to them that they were shortening everyone's life with their cooperation.

The tall blond teenager, Val, must have thought things through.

Manny Noris said in an impatient voice, "Val, slow down. That's the second time you've botched the entry code."

White caught on instantly. He strode over to Val Tredgett's chair and jerked it away from the computer.

"You're through. Get over there with the two programmers where we can keep an eye on you." The KGB agent turned to Ursula. "You use this computer. If you make as many mistakes as this lout, I'll have your hands cut off."

"No one uses my computer but me," Val roared.

His sudden rebellion caught White by surprise. Val stood up abruptly, causing his chair to topple over backward. He snatched up his computer housing and smashed it down on Noris's monitor so hard that the monitor case cracked and the video tube smashed. When Val threw his computer back onto the table, loose parts rattled inside.

Lao found it hard to suppress her grin. Those hackers had both brains and guts. She glanced around to see if there were any way she could prevent him from being killed. It seemed impossible. White had cautiously put the two programmers as far from the hackers as he could.

She reconsidered the battle positions. She was removed from the scene of action, but that meant the three terrorists had to divide their attention between the hackers and her. The time had come to risk everything in a desperate gamble. She eased forward in her chair, transferring her weight to her feet.

White grabbed Val by the shoulders and sent him spinning away from the computers. Tredgett towered three inches over the Russian, but he weighed thirty-five pounds less and hadn't been trained by the KGB. Val tried to use his long legs to snap a kick to the shorter man's crotch. White easily countered and grabbed the foot, dumping Tredgett on his back.

Lao slid off her chair, only to have a guard put a single bullet in the floor at her feet. They knew enough to watch her carefully, and from a distance.

It was Olga who saved Val from being beaten to death. She called out, "I've got it! I've got control of the computer. What do I do now?"

White booted Val in the shoulder as the lad tried rolling to his feet. Then the KGB agent hurried to protect Glitch's computer before someone could smash it.

Val came to his feet, determined to charge White. Tredgett didn't seem to care if his actions got him killed or not.

"Val!" Lao barked.

He stopped and glanced at her. She shook her head and indicated he should stay where he was. The more she got people spread around the large room, the harder it would be for the guards to eliminate them all.

"Are you lying?" White demanded of Olga Giltch. "If you are, I'll break Tredgett's bones."

She was pale but determined. "See for yourself."

"You show me. Can you put these instructions for reprogramming the computer on one of its own terminals?"

"You mean the mainframe? That would give us away."

"That's all right," White said soothingly. "Just prove you can do it."

The entire room waited in absolute quiet as the pretty thirteen-year-old made the necessary entries.

A moment later, she said, "It's done. Now what?"

"Now we wait," White told her.

Lao looked for a way to reach the guards, but she was being watched too closely.

Four minutes later Olga said, "Something's happening. There's a message on this screen. It says, 'Control established.' What does that mean?"

White laughed. "It means that our Russian scientists can now manage without you. I have a special reward for you, and there's a bed down the hall."

He grabbed her wrist and dragged her to the door.

"Kill the rest of them," he told the guards.

13

Gadgets snatched his Mac-10 from its leg clip before the scrambling card players reached their Kalashnikovs. It was equipped with a Mac suppressor, which, unlike other silencers, didn't slow bullets below the speed of sound. Instead it rechanneled the gases, slowing them down. As the Stony Man warrior hosed the terrorists, the bullets crackled like snapping whips, but the gun itself made little noise.

Gadgets managed to cut down three of the enemy, but had to dive and roll as the fourth brought his assault rifle around, firing all the way. The terrorist emptied the clip after Gadgets as he rolled. The 30-round clip used by the Kalashnikov lasts only three seconds when the trigger is held down, but that can seem like three hours when a person is trying to dodge the bullets.

When the bolt on the Russian rifle stopped in the open position, Gadgets brought his Ingram around as the terrorist dropped his weapon and dived for a Kalashnikov his comrades in gore would no longer need.

Gadgets knew not many bullets remained, but he'd been using the Ingram on automatic and not on cyclic fire. The cyclic fire spit bullets twice as fast as the Kalashnikovs, but automatic was a mere 96 rounds per minute. He hoped only that he'd been left with enough ammunition to finish the firefight. He'd never have time to reload.

Steadying himself, Gadgets brought the subgun around, but the terrorist had snatched another assault rifle and rolled behind a car. Gadgets sprang to his feet, bullets snapping around his ankles as the terrorist shot under the car.

Gadgets ran two steps and leapt to the top of an old kitchen table, still strewn with playing cards. From his new position, neither he nor the Free PR killer had a line of sight on the other. Before Gadgets could change to a more stable position, a short burst from the Kalashnikov chopped away a table leg. Then the lights went out.

Gadgets fell partway with the table, then pushed off in a dive and roll, trying to put something else between himself and the killer as the lights returned and the short bursts ranged closer. A bullet nicked the heel of his shoe as he took another dive over the hood of the terrorist's cover.

As he slid across the hood of the old Pontiac, Gadgets aimed his Ingram down. A .45 smashed the butt of the Kalashnikov and then the Ingram's bolt locked open. The clip was empty.

When Gadgets's bullet hit the stock, the terrorist jerked his rifle to one side. He began to swing his weapon back in line as Gadgets flew over his head. When Gadgets came to his feet, the terrorist was facing him, grinning. The Kalashnikov was pointed at Gadgets's head. From three feet away there wasn't much chance the killer would miss.

The goon's grin splashed. Some of the gore sprayed Gadgets. Then came the distinctive boom of Ironman's big Python as the terrorist collapsed to the floor. Ironman stood by the closed door in a classic dueling stance. The big piece in his hand seemed to stretch halfway across the huge garage.

"I thought this was going to be a quiet recon," he said. "I could hear those Kalashnikovs fifty yards away."

"Good, you joined the party just when it was threatening to become a drag," Gadgets answered as he slammed a fresh clip into the Ingram. "Everyone else seems to be in the one barracks. Seeing we've been announced, we may as well include them in the celebrations."

Lyons nodded, put the Python back in shoulder leather and unslung the Konzak. "Let's waltz," he answered as he headed back out the door.

Gadgets and Ironman moved slowly, cautiously, listening for reaction, waiting for their eyes to once again adjust to the dark.

Two sets of boots thumped toward them.

One goon called to another, "What was that?"

"Probably those card-playing assholes living it up again," the other replied.

Gadgets returned the Ingram to its leg clip and unleathered the silenced Beretta 93-R. The shooting in the Quonset hut had caused only this small reaction. Able Team needed as much surprise as they could muster.

Gadgets and Lyons froze. The two terror goons almost walked right into the warriors in camou fatigues. The Beretta was less than two feet from the side of a terrorist's head when it whispered death in his ear.

The second man felt the first stumble and whirled in time to see the slight muzzle flash from the 93-R. The 115-grain parabellum scrambled the brain while it was still trying to interpret what the eye had registered.

Lyons fished out his communicator and spoke into it quietly, telling Blancanales to bring the van up to the buildings. He was unsure how quickly they'd have to retreat.

As the two Stony Man warriors started toward the occupied building once more, Gadgets murmured, "Something's wrong."

"Too few enemy," Lyons confirmed in a soft voice.

They reached a door at one end of the barracks and split to check for sentries. They moved cautiously to the corners of the building and back.

Gadgets shook his head—*nothing*. Lyons nodded to tell him the coast was clear.

Lyons stayed by the door while Gadgets entered, Ingram ready to contest occupancy of the hall. Gadgets moved stealthily to the first door, then signaled for Lyons to advance.

Quietly shutting the outside door, Lyons moved to the other side of the door.

When his back was covered, Gadgets slowly turned the doorknob. Standard procedure was to kick in the door and move in quickly, but Able Team wished to preserve their advantage of surprise as long as possible.

The room was empty. Gadgets covered Lyons from the doorway as he moved up the hall to the next door. Things were oddly quiet in the old building. Muffled voices drifted down the hall, but the Able Team warriors couldn't tell where they originated.

They were checking the third empty room, when heavy autofire rattled from a room farther up the hall. In response two sets of boots clattered down the hall.

If there were prisoners anyplace, they'd be in the room where the firing was occurring. Ironman and Gadgets burst from the room they were checking, determined to save what lives they could.

The two terrorists running down the hall from the other direction expected further reinforcements. By the time they realized the two men charging toward them weren't on the same team it was too late. Gadgets's suppressed Mac-10 opened up on full cyclic fire. His figure eight cut them almost into halves.

Gadgets slammed in a fresh magazine and sprinted to catch up to Ironman. The firing in the room was heavy and led them to believe they were too late to do more than demand retribution.

WHEN WHITE ORDERED THE GUARDS to kill four of the hackers, Knight and Lao, the latter was the first to react. She slid from her chair, holding on to its back, then spun and launched the chair in a high arc toward White. She knew the chair would not hit anyone; that wasn't her intention.

The terrorists watched the high flight of the chair. White yanked on Giltch's arm as he easily sidestepped the chair. Only two pair of eyes didn't follow it to its destination. Lao used the reactive force from throwing the chair to hurtle herself in the other direction. Donald Knight knew a break when he saw it. He leapt from his own chair and launched it in another direction.

Olga Giltch was too young to have thought much about getting killed, but the precocious thirteen-year-old had spent fourteen months of puberty dreaming of romance. Fred White fulfilled none of those dreams. When White yanked her arm as he dodged out of the way of the chair, Olga accepted the pull and added her own push to it. She crashed into White's stomach with all the force her eighty-five pounds could generate.

Already White was slightly off balance. The attack from an unexpected source sent him staggering. He let go of Olga and flailed his arms before regaining control. Then he produced a small automatic from his jacket pocket.

The terrorist who'd been watching Lao so closely was the first to wrench his eyes from the distracting flight of the chair. He knew Lao was the most dangerous, and brought the Kalashnikov to bear on her but held his fire. By that time she was directly between two guards, neither of whom could shoot for fear of hitting the other.

The third terrorist watched the chair hit the floor and bounce. By then Knight was coming at him in a long, low dive. The assault rifle sprayed over Knight's head. Then the tackle connected and both men crashed to the floor.

The terrorist Lao was attacking tried to shoot her legs out from under her. Lao saw the rifle swing into position and launched herself into a flying kick. She didn't believe in flying kicks; they left the martial artist in the air too long. But the bullets whipping under her had given her no choice.

Lao's foot snapped forward with the force of a piston on a steam locomotive. Her boot drove into the gunman's chest, slamming him back against a wall. Lao landed on her feet and used her momentum to plant her small fist into the sternum exactly where she had kicked. The breastbone broke.

As her target crumpled, Lao presented a clear shot to the terrorist who'd been following her with the sights of his Kalashnikov. Before he squeezed the trigger, Manny and Zorro, working in concert, tackled him. The bullets chewed up the floor.

Knight managed to distract the third guard in time to keep him from firing on the young people. The guard let the stock slide from under his arm and rammed it into Knight's stomach. Then he swung the barrel until it touched the soldier's head. Before he fired, however, Ursula's nails raked across his face and Val kicked him behind the knee.

The terrorist managed to remain standing and swung his rifle butt again, taking Val out with a blow to the plexis. Then he snapped the barrel into U.U.'s chest, sending her staggering across the room. Knight was still on the floor, gasping for air. Once more the terrorist stopped using his gun as a club, and swung the end of the barrel back toward the soldier's head.

White had seen enough. He didn't take time to use his ineffective handgun. He strode to the door, yanked it open and yelled, "Guards," at the top of his lungs.

His shout brought immediate results. A big guy with an assault shotgun stepped through the door. Then the gun spit out flame and steel balls. White's head sprayed across the wall ten feet behind him.

The booming Konzak froze everyone in the room except Lao. She'd been expecting Able Team, anyway. She brought up the assault rifle taken from the goon with the crushed chest and squeezed the trigger, blasting the head from the terrorist who was about to deal with Manny and Zorro.

Gadgets moved around White's headless body before it could fall. His Ingram bellowed. The terrorist who shot Knight froze at the unnerving boom of Lyons's big weapon. Blood bubbled out of his chest and neck and he collapsed.

Lyons watched the door, demanding, "Where are the rest of the troops?"

"How many did you eliminate outside?" Lao asked.

"Nine," Gadgets told her.

"Good chance you have them all. The main force has taken a government site of some sort."

"Project Hot Shot!" Lyons exclaimed. "We have to stop them. They could wipe out the entire country."

"Too late," Lao answered. "They have control of the site and the computer."

"How do you know?"

Lao filled in the Able Team warrior. Her words were calm, carefully chosen and succinct. Lyons had a full update in less than two minutes. When the briefing was over, he had two questions.

"You got them into the computer from here?"

Lao nodded.

"Can you delay them from here?"

Lao thought for a second, her face blank.

It was Knight who interrupted with, "Executive prerogative!"

Lyons cocked an eyebrow at him.

The Army programmer explained, excitement creeping into his voice, "All our big weapons have provision for the President to issue a code word that aborts the weapon. He phones the code word to the site and the base commander enters it. If these young people can crack the computer so easily, maybe we can figure out the abort command."

Lyons turned to the hackers. "You game?"

They all nodded.

Ursula said, "We have only two computers left."

Manny Noris started pulling tools from his pockets. "I can put together a third from the wrecks."

"You needed here?" Lyons asked Lao.

"They need protection. They don't need my computer knowledge."

Lyons turned to Gadgets, "Get Blancanales in here, armed for bear."

Gadgets pulled out his communicator and started talking. Four hackers moved back to their computers, following Knight, who was explaining his plan to them. Noris was already gathering up the smashed computers.

Blancanales entered, carrying his favorite M-16/M-203 combination and five bandoliers of ammunition. "Where's the war zone?" he asked.

"You have protective custody of these people," Lyons told him. "If they don't succeed with their computers, the United States is the war zone."

"And the rest of you?"

"We're going to see what we can do at the missile site."

Blancanales's face fell. "Without me?"

"Everything depends on these hackers," Lyons told him. "Someone has to protect them. You choose."

Blancanales nodded glumly. He knew Lao was fit and he wasn't, but he had to fight to keep his face impassive. By the time he was finished nodding, the rest of the team was out the door.

"Vaya con Dios," he muttered. Suddenly he felt ancient, expendable.

14

Lyons drove the van the 130 miles to the secret missile site in the Monongahela National Forest. It took him one hour and five minutes.

Gadgets spent some of that time on a radio relay through Stony Man. The rest of the time he and Lao concentrated on hanging on and keeping their mouths shut. Both Ironman and Blancanales could move the van at a speed just under a rocket's escape velocity from Earth. However, Blancanales's passengers were less apt to suffer heart attacks while in transit at a slower speed.

Gadgets tried without success to reach Hal Brognola at Stony Man. Katz, back from a mission with Phoenix Force, took over the task of having the various police forces clear the road for the hurtling van. Aaron "The Bear" Kurtzman worked on locating Brognola.

Kurtzman found the Stony Man chief of ops at the White House, where he'd been summoned to a hastily arranged conference on the terrorist takeover of Project Hot Shot.

Brognola ordered Able Team's call patched through to him at the Oval Office. In the background Gadgets could hear the President telling someone, "I don't know how they get on to these things so fast. Ask Hal."

Gadgets quickly briefed Brognola. He wasn't as terse as Lyons or Lao, but his explanations required less figuring out.

"You've been on the speaker phone," Brognola told Gadgets when he'd finished. "Hold on while we discuss this."

The line went silent while the President and his closest advisers discussed the situation.

Lyons turned around. "What's happening with Hal?" he asked.

"I can hear you almost as well if you speak to the windshield," Gadgets answered. "I lose the thread of my thought when you turn around to talk."

Lyons shrugged as he burned rubber through an S curve on a steep descent.

When they straightened out, Lyons shouted without turning his head, "So what does Hal say?"

"I don't know yet. He has us on hold."

Lyons's head jerked around. "He what?"

Gadgets suddenly turned pale; Lyons pivoted his head back in time to avoid rear-ending a police cruiser. The cruiser had its siren screaming, clearing the highway for Able Team. Lyons nipped the van around the cruiser and allowed it to slowly fall behind. It was the fourth police escort to be left behind in this way.

Gadgets called to Lyons, "Hal's back now. I'll fill you in in a moment."

Hal waited until he had Gadgets's full attention, then told him, "The President has had great faith in your abilities."

Gadgets interrupted with, "That's just because Ironman's never taken him for a ride."

Hal paused to make sure the interruption was over before continuing, "General Hofstetter's in charge. The President's talking to him right now. He'll cooperate with whatever you want to do."

"Hold on a mo," Gadgets answered. He relayed the message to Lyons.

"Why and why?" Lyons answered.

Gadgets relayed the questions to Brognola. "Ironman wants to know why we're being given so much discretion and why Hofstetter's in charge."

"I told you. The President has faith in you."

"Uh, I don't think Carl will accept gratitude as a political motive."

"I'm not going to cause embarrassment by relaying the questions. You'll have to accept my informed guesses."

Gadgets braced himself as they swerved past yet another screaming police car. "Shoot," he told Brognola.

"You're the only ones who know what's happening. All the agencies have been caught napping. Hofstetter's the ideal man for this sort of thing. He's flexible, manipulative and tricky, but he never passes the buck and he always accepts responsibility for what he does. The President doesn't have to dot the *i*s and cross the *t*s. Alan will do *whatever* is necessary."

"I've got the message. Thanks."

Gadgets closed down communications and then shouted to Lyons over the roar of the van, "Hal thinks we're being given our head because we're doing okay so far. But he says to watch out for Hofstetter. He'll wipe us if he can see an advantage in it."

"Hal says things so subtly I can never figure what he's telling us," Lyons answered.

Lyons had the sharpest mind Gadgets had ever encountered. The Able Team leader was a brilliant strategist who could improvise a campaign that would confound Machiavelli. But when it came to conversation, Lyons was about as subtle as the Konzak he carried into battle.

General Hofstetter had mobilized all the helicopters at Bolling Air Force Base and had control of the recreation area before Able Team arrived. The van was waved through to command headquarters, which was simply a tent pitched within sight of the missile launcher disguised as a water tower. Hofstetter took them to a table covered with maps and diagrams that had been set up outside the tent.

"There are only two entrances," he told Able Team, "both cut from solid rock. A handful of men can hold off thousands under those conditions." He indicated the entrances on a map.

"They managed to fight their way in," Gadgets said.

"Place was poorly defended. The idea of not having it seem guarded was a lousy one. They're well armed, holding hostages and expecting us. There's the added problem that the administration doesn't want the nature of the weapon known. I'm supposed to deal with this before the press gets hold of it."

Lyons gave a derisive snort of laughter.

"They're holding out the threat of going to the press. So far they haven't done that," Hofstetter insisted.

"They will," Lyons told him. "Terrorism doesn't work without publicity."

"I dislike having my nose rubbed in the obvious," the general snapped back.

"Then don't spout nonsense. I suppose you cut the telephone lines."

"You suppose correctly." Hofstetter's voice was cold, formal.

"Then how do they intend to notify the press when they're ready?"

For the first time Hofstetter seemed puzzled.

NOT ALL THE MEMBERS of the Puerto Rican Bird-Watching Society attacked the Project Hot Shot complex. Ten of them drifted through the woods and up the mountain as ordered by Ignacio Quadra. They were to monitor the United

States's reaction and coordinate the external events. What Quadra didn't order—he didn't even know it was happening—was for the terrorists to meet another eight KGB specialists on the mountain.

From a boulder-strewn ledge, Yepes Rivera used his 10x50 binoculars to watch Able Team confer with Hofstetter in front of the command tent. The huge terrorist had exchanged his jeans and bare feet for camou fatigues and combat boots. With the change of clothing came a change of psyche. Rivera was no longer the brute jailer but a respected field commander.

His job was complex, but he'd been training for it since the day he'd entered Patrice Lumumba fifteen years earlier. Of course, at that time they didn't know the exact target. They did know Rivera would help Quadra become a ruthless terrorist, a person who enjoyed death for its own sake. He'd then be used to turn one of the Americans' own missiles against them.

Rivera knew that at that moment Russian scientists were working in the underground complex to reprogram the missile to take out New York City. Quadra thought they were collecting proof of American involvement in bacterial warfare. Rivera regretted in advance what the destruction of New York would do to Quadra's self image. But he expected that Quadra would not live long enough to deny his complicity.

At the right time Rivera would inform the world press what was happening at Seneca Rock. But he would wait until the evacuation. He had to get the Russians out of sight before the press got wind of the story. As far as the rest of the world was concerned, the destruction would be entirely the work of the Puerto Rican independence movement.

The thought made Rivera laugh. The Puerto Ricans were so content with their status as a United States territory that it had taken years to round up enough psychopaths and killers to get Free PR on its feet. But the world would buy yet another tale of American imperialism. Uncle Sam's behavior in Central America made selling such ridiculous stories extremely easy.

Rivera's moody thoughts were interrupted by a Puerto Rican henchman: "General Quadra is on the radio, sir."

Long practice enabled Rivera to keep his face neutral. He found Quadra's choice of title pretentious and ludicrous. Without moving from his prone lookout position, Rivera accepted the handset from the terrorist.

"Sí, mi general," Rivera said sarcastically into the handset.

Quadra ignored the jest from the man he thought of as his friend. "Yepes, we've got trouble down here."

"What kind of trouble?"

"The technicians. Old White did his part. We got instructions on the screen showing us how to access the computer. But these Russian idiots tried something with the program instead of simply collecting data as they were supposed to do. Now the computer is doing odd things. They can't finish their programming and they can't get the data, either. They're going to throw off our entire schedule."

"Have you tried White?"

"What for? He'll have vanished by now."

Rivera, who knew his fellow KGB agent's sexual proclivities, thought now. There was a good chance that at least one hacker was still alive to clear up the mess.

"Don't sweat it," he told Quadra. "They're good technicians. I'd want to control the program before I went for information. You never know what sort of booby traps are in there that'll wipe the memory if they're triggered."

Rivera had no idea of the truth. He spoke to keep things calm, if he possibly could.

Before Quadra could object Rivera continued, "If you need more time, I'll buy it for you. Don't worry. In the meantime, I'll see what can be done about finding help for the techs. Anything else?"

"No. You've relieved my mind."

"That's what lieutenants are for. I'll be out of contact several hours, but don't sweat it."

Rivera returned the handset to the waiting terrorist. Then he pulled back from the edge of the rock before standing up. "Round up the men. We have to get back to base fast," he ordered.

"What about our surveillance here?"

"It'll keep until we get back."

Even as he jogged down the slope to the hidden transport Rivera was calculating the time for the two-way trip. He decided it wouldn't hurt to let the authorities stew for four hours. By then he'd be back with any of the kids who were left alive at the base.

"FOR A GUY who wanted to see us dead, you're not too bad," Manny Noris told Knight.

The Army programmer had the grace to blush. "I didn't realize you were trying to slow things down."

"Dr. Lao wasn't sure you could be trusted."

The feeling had been mutual. Knight changed the subject. "The computer you patched together seems to be working fine. That gives us three personals."

Val interrupted, "Those guys on the mainframe will wise up. Soon they'll know we're interfering. Then all they have to do is disconnect the modem."

"All we can do is stall, unless we figure a way to scramble the other program."

"Easy," Olga told him, "but they'd catch on before we did any real damage. We're trying not to noticeably alter the computer responses. We're just slowing it down by feeding it irrelevant data.'' She dropped her voice and added, ''What gives with that old guy with the white hair? I wish he'd sit down. He gives me the creeps.''

''I don't think he's that old. He's just got white hair,'' Knight answered. ''And judging from the bandage on his neck, he's been wounded recently.''

''But what's he doing?'' Ursula asked.

The group watched Blancanales as he cut firing slots in the hoardings over the windows. Earlier he'd gone around the camp and collected all the old junk he could find and dumped it in the hall. From one end to the other, the main hall was now filled with old bed frames, bed springs, miscellaneous office furniture and short lengths of barbed wire stolen from a nearby pasture.

''He's preparing to defend us against attack,'' Knight told Giltch.

''We're safe now, aren't we?''

''I'd think so, but he seems the cautious type.''

''Besides,'' Val asked, ''what good would one man be against a large attack?''

Knight smiled. ''I have some experience, you know.''

''Okay. What good are two men against an attack?''

''You saw how easily those three burst in here. Not much good in a place like this.''

''I thought as much,'' Val mused. ''I wonder—''

Whatever Val Tredgett wondered remained unspoken.

Zorro interrupted with, ''I think our interference has been discovered.''

15

"Horseshit!" Lyons rumbled. "There's got to be a way into that missile site. How do they get their air, water? Where's the sewage go? How did they get the missile and the computer in there?"

"We didn't truck the damn weapon here for the world to see." Hofstetter's voice was as frosty as Lyons's was hot. "The shell was built inside the tank. Other components were small enough to be trollied through the tunnels. The computer components went through the main tunnels easily."

"Air and water?"

"Dozens of small vents, designed so none are large enough to gas the place quickly. Besides, these terrorists used gas themselves and have masks. Water comes from the site's own artesian wells. No access from the surface."

"That leaves sewage."

"There's a stream just around the curve of the mountain. It leads to the Cheat River. A tunnel was put through the mountain to empty the sewage into the stream. It enters behind a falls."

"Untreated?" Gadgets asked.

"What do you expect? Us to announce the installation by putting a treatment plant on the stream?"

"Shit! Literally shit!" Gadgets said. "By the time you guys are finished saving the country, it won't be fit to live in."

"Later," Ironman told Gadgets. "How big is that sewage conduit, General?"

Hofstetter, caught by surprise, turned to his charts. About three minutes later he said, "From the scale of the plan, I'd guess it's about two feet in diameter."

"Drilled through solid rock?"

"I remember we had a hell of a time with the drilling. Had to be done from inside the site and the stuff hauled out as garbage. At least, when we blasted out the original complex the recreation area was closed on some pretext."

"What's the flow-through?"

"Heavy. Those artesian wells really spurt the water out this time of year. It goes straight to the drainage cistern. When the water's used to flush a toilet or something it's diverted. Then it rejoins the flow."

"Good. Cuts the heat problems. We'll need dry suits, full-face scuba masks, a selection of eight-cube air tanks filled to 3,700 pounds, climbers' boots, good nylon rope and about fifty instant-dry neoprene patching kits. We'll also need flashlights with at least four hours of life and an ultrasmall diver's torch with preset regulators and gauges off. How soon can we have them?"

"That shaft's too long to crawl up. It slopes uphill all the way and there's a large volume of water pouring down it," the general protested.

"Got a better idea?" Lyons asked.

"Not yet."

"Then start the stuff moving. I want it here in case you don't come up with something better."

Gadgets and Lao had been listening to Lyons's list.

"We need throat mikes," Gadgets said.

Lao asked, "How big is that tunnel exactly?"

The general searched around until he found a small ruler, which he applied to a blueprint.

"Thirty inches."

Lao said, "Make sure there's ample 11 mm waterproof Perlon rope, two pair of climbers' gloves each, hammer and pitons and one hundred feet of extra air line."

"Why?" asked Lyons.

"You ever mountain-climbed?"

Lyons shook his head.

"I go first. You carry my tank. No other way."

"Are you sure you know what you're doing?" Hofstetter asked Lao.

"If she didn't she wouldn't have spoken," Lyons answered.

The general summoned an aide, who took down the list of demands. The officer knew what he was doing. When the list was complete, he went over it again, checking with Able Team on sizes, quantities, specifications.

At one point the aide asked, "Fifty patching kits?"

"A few more, if you can get them. If you can figure a way to speed drying, get that, too."

The officer made more notes and was still shaking his head when he called over a soldier with communications gear.

Without saying anything else, Able Team started up the side of the mountain.

"Where are you going?" Hofstetter asked.

Gadgets turned and answered, "We're finding a quiet spot to sleep. Call us when the stuff gets here."

Hofstetter thrived on emergencies. He figured that was what the armed forces were for. He thought little of Able Team's plan. It was impossible to get through a third of a mile of conduit, against flowing water, fighting uphill all the way. Even if they achieved the impossible, they'd be in no shape to take on forty or fifty terrorists.

But it was a plan, and he could find none better.

The Navy was able to supply the diving gear and assemble the torch demanded. Their entire supply of repair kits, including those rounded up from their divers, came to forty-three. The climbing gear was purchased at a specialty store in New York. It would be paradropped by an Air Force jet.

All the materials reached their position in two hours and fourteen minutes. Hofstetter was proud of his officers' efficiency. He went to find Able Team.

The two warriors and Lao had gone two hundred yards up the mountain, where they had bedded down on loose humus from the cedar forest. From their breathing Hofstetter was sure they were sound asleep. However, when he was within fifty feet of them, three pairs of eyes opened and regarded him calmly.

When Hofstetter was close enough to speak without raising his voice, he said, "Your ordnance is here. I still think it won't work."

The three stood up and stretched. Lyons holstered the big Python; he'd been sleeping with it in his fist.

"Won't hurt to take a look," Gadgets said.

"I had someone find you a high-protein meal."

"Good thinking," Lyons acknowledged.

The general was surprised at how much the compliment affected him. Why had he come to wake them himself? Why hadn't he sent a soldier? He had to admit to himself that he liked being around these people. Their competence seemed to spill over on those around them.

Hofstetter and the aide who'd supervised gathering the gear sipped coffees while the warriors silently demolished plates of steak and eggs.

"What can we do to help?" the aide asked.

"Get three soldiers to help with the patching kits," Lyons answered. "What news from the jackals?"

"Nothing. We called in once. They told us they'd call us when they wanted to talk."

The three Able Team members exchanged uneasy glances.

It took an hour to prepare. They put on the dry suits and bent and contorted while soldiers used the patching kits to add wads of extra material to knees, elbows and other parts of the suits that would be scraping against the rock. Lyons carried two sets of air tanks. From the tank on his left shoulder, sixty-five feet of hose ran to Lao's regulator.

Strapped to her chest, Lao carried the small torch with cutting head. Dangling from her belt were a hammer and a bag of pitons, and dangling from a special belt loop, a hundred feet of knotted nylon rope. With a patching kit a flashlight had been affixed to the top of her face mask.

Lyons's Konzak and Python plus bandoliers of ammunition were slung in a waterproof pack between the two tanks on his back.

"Lord!" the aide exclaimed. "No man can crawl through a small tunnel with that much on his back."

"Yeah," Gadgets agreed. "It's a good thing we've got Ironman."

Gadgets was also heavily loaded. He carried the arms and munitions for both himself and Lao. The two bags straddled a large eight-cubic-foot tank. The three of them would have overjoyed the casting director for *Star Wars*.

Gadgets did a check of their communicators. The throat mikes under the tight collars of the dry suits gave voices a gravel quality and the hissing of the mouthpieces made them all sound like Darth Vader, but communications were clear. An all-terrain vehicle transported them to the falls. Hofstetter rode with them.

The small waterfall was postcard perfect. It had been created that way. Face masks in place and air on, Able Team waded under it, staggering from the impact of the water.

Just behind the main flow of the falls, they found a circular hole cut in the rock. The opening was only a few inches larger around than the heavily laden Ironman.

The relentless cascade of water, filling less than twenty percent of the tunnel, rushed from the cistern like the flood from an open hydrant.

Lao turned on her lantern and let the coiled, knotted rope fall. One end remained tied to her belt.

"Wait," she commanded.

Lyons grabbed her by the hips and raised her over his head. His hands were about two feet into the channel. Lao bent her knees until her boots found a grip just inside the opening. Bracing her back against the other side of the tube, she groped blindly until her fingers found a small fault, then pulled herself free of Ironman's support.

When she had pulled herself as high as she could, she braced her back against the wall and searched for new toeholds. The steady flow of cold water added a relentless pressure against her climb. The cold threatened to numb her fingers through the tough gloves.

Slowly, fighting for every toe and fingerhold, Lao struggled upward. At this point the tunnel rose at a sixty-degree angle. The climb wasn't as difficult as straight up, but the relentless pressure of the water more than made up for that.

They could manage without tanks and face masks, but didn't dare leave them off because the sewage was bound to leave pockets of gas devoid of air. They wouldn't know they were in trouble until it was too late.

Lao found a place where a fault in the rock provided two secure footholds. She reached as high as she could and drove a piton into each side of the tunnel. Inching up until she was standing on those pitons, she drove in two more. When she was standing on the second set of pitons, she drove in a fifth one, just over her head. She let the hammer hang from her belt and brought up the rope she was dragging and tied it to the fifth piton without taking the end from her belt.

She no longer felt chilled. She was breathing hard from the exertion. The air regulator seemed to fight her for every breath of air she took. The rope was heavy with water, and dragging all that air line was almost as bad as being encumbered by fifty pounds of air and tanks. Sweat rolled down her face inside the mask.

"You can start up now," she panted. Her throat microphone picked up her words and the radio relayed them back to Lyons and Schwarz.

Lyons tested the rope and began the hand-over-hand climb that would take him to the pitons right under Lao.

Gadgets waited for Lyons to finish his climb, then followed. When he was directly under Lyons, Lao told him about the footholds.

Lao sighed, flexed her arms and began the next sixty feet of ascent. It would take thirty of these relays to reach the end of the tunnel. Already her shoulders were trying to tell her this was hard work. The rock felt greased where the water perpetually ran over it. The controlled breathing, in through the mouth and out through the nose, was the opposite to her martial-arts breathing and required both concentration and exertion. But there would be no turning back now.

Beginning the fourth ascent, Lao came to a crossed mesh of steel rods. They'd been set in concrete trowled smooth with the rock wall. She reported her findings on the radio.

"Set pitons and use the torch," Lyons told her.

As Lao worked, Gadgets said, "I've got questions."

Lyons grunted.

"How did you know we'd need the torch? How did they manage to put those bars in at this point?"

"Would you put an unrestricted tunnel in straight to the heart of your complex?" Lyons countered.

"What would have happened if you couldn't cut it with a torch?"

"Would have had to set explosive, back right out, set it off and try again."

"How did they install that?"

"Dunno. Probably a cave above they could lower workmen into."

"How do you figure that?" Gadgets persisted.

"You never run out of questions?"

"Why do you ask?" Gadgets countered.

Lyons gave up. "Angle's wrong."

Gadgets had to think about it. "You figure the tunnel would miss the complex if it continued at this angle?"

Ironman gave an affirmative grunt.

Four years of water and sewage had corroded the steel. Otherwise the small torch would not have held enough acetylene and oxygen for the job. Lao cut the bars at the top of the grate, where they were clear of the water, and weakened them in the underwater spots enough to bend them out of the way.

The oxygen ran out while the torch was out of the water. Lao's lamp didn't show what was beyond the destroyed grating. With the last orange gasp of acetylene flame she raised the torch.

The resulting explosion blasted her off the pitons.

16

"Gather up all the weapons and ammunition you can find," Knight told Val Tredgett.

Val nodded at Blancanales. "He's already done it."

Zared "Zorro" Elvy had just announced that their attempts to stop the Russians from taking over the Project Hot Shot computer had been detected.

Knight found himself shaken by his own reactions. He had reacted as a military man before reacting as a programmer. Until that moment, he'd always thought of himself primarily as a programmer and secondarily as a soldier. Knight was surprised to find the soldier foremost—and chagrined to discover the soldier to be inadequate. He had thought of the weapons only when it appeared he'd have to use them. The white-haired warrior had gathered them as a matter of prudence.

The warrior was looking at them now, listening to the conversation. On impulse Knight asked him, "What now?"

"First, the desperate blow," Blancanales said.

"'The desperate blow'?"

"Assume these young people know what they're talking about. They have until now. You've been detected. What single blow can you launch to cripple them before they unplug the modem?"

Knight slapped himself on the forehead and joined the stampede to the computers. Blancanales had spoken loudly, wanting everyone in the room to hear him.

"Abort code!" Glitch shouted.

"We'd never find it in time," Val argued. "Juggle the stored data."

"I *can* find the abort code," Olga insisted.

Elvy, Noris and Giltch were at the three working computers. Knight snapped out commands to them, utilizing their strong points in an attempt to land the desperate blow.

He turned to the hacker who thought like a businessman. "Zorro, set up a time-sharing arrangement on that modem. I want all three computers to get their instructions in."

Elvy nodded and started working. It was standard business practice for a mainframe to accept commands from several terminals at once. He'd have the instructions in place in seconds.

"Manny, you and Val figure out how much memory damage you can do in twenty seconds, then do it."

Manny raised an eyebrow at Val, who said, "Let's add Goto glitches all over the place. Keep them going in circles."

"You figure them. I'll enter," Noris replied.

Knight turned to Giltch, whose fingers were already flying over her keyboard. He didn't need to tell Olga her assignment. She told him.

"The code's got to be easy to remember and fast to use. There's a pattern of using words that mean hot and heat in the main commands."

"The computers are all acting as time-sharing terminals," Zorro reported.

"Monitor," Knight ordered. "Call out the progress on both sides."

It had been close to sixty seconds since the Russians had discovered something was interfering with their attempts to reprogram the Hot Shot mainframe.

"They're still wasting time looking for the source of the interference," Zorro said.

Knight raised an eyebrow at Ursula, who'd been looking over Zorro's shoulder. She nodded.

Knight had no idea how the hackers could deduce that so quickly, but the Army programmer believed them. Kids who grew up with computers worked almost by instinct. What Knight had to do by calculation, they did by feeling.

"Ten phony reroute commands implanted," Zorro reported as Knight stepped over to where Blancanales was standing and watching.

"What's to be done?" Knight asked. "I assume they'll figure out we're alive and well and send killers to do something to remedy the situation."

"I've done what I can think of," Blancanales answered. "Why don't you inspect and suggest?"

Zorro shouted, "We've been disconnected."

Olga followed that with, "Damn! I had the answer. I just didn't get it entered. The code is 'Cool Down.'"

"Okay, everybody, good going," Blancanales said. "Now we prepare for a hot war."

"Let's just get the hell out of here," Knight growled.

"Listen," Blancanales said, his voice reflecting his weariness.

They all paused. Then they heard what Blancanales heard. Not far off, someone was barking something in a foreign language. No one needed to understand the language to know he was giving orders to troops.

LAO'S BODY STOPPED most of the downward force of the blast. Lyons was almost deafened by the explosion, but felt little of the shock wave. However, he did feel the air hose and climbing rope coiling slackly around him.

Lyons bent his knees, scraping the tanks against the other side of the drilled tunnel, wedging himself even more firmly in place. His arms extended upward just in time to catch Lao.

Ironman's mighty arms absorbed some of the shock, but stopping the falling body drove him even tighter into his wedged position.

Ironman unfolded Lao's knees from his chest and moved her into a position where she could breath. He snapped off the light on her mask, fished out his own and shone it on her. She was unconscious. Her face mask was askew, and she was no longer drawing air from the mouthpiece.

Gadgets's calm voice came over the communicator earphone. "What happened? Who can answer?"

"Explosion up above. Lao fell. Unconscious. I think alive, but mouth off respirator."

"Can you reach her mouth with yours?"

Lyons struggled for a few seconds, then reported, "Can't move. Wedged."

"Can you reach the buckles on the tank harness?" Gadgets asked.

Lyons turned off his light and returned it to his belt. Then he rearranged Lao's unconscious form so her feet rested on his knees and her behind sat on his head. He steadied her with one hand while the other found the buckle.

"Can do," he told Gadgets.

"Okay. Take off your mask, then let the tanks go. I'll hold them. Try mouth-to-mouth with Lao using her respirator. It has enough line to reach."

Lyons quickly slung off his mask. The rushing, cold water was a shock on his sweaty face. With one hand he released the harness buckles, supporting Lao with the other.

Still holding his breath, Lyons turned Lao until her feet were on his knees, toes pointing toward him, and her head rested on top of his. He held her hips away from him. Then he gave a tremendous heave with his legs, hoping Lao had sank her pitons well.

At first it seemed he was too firmly wedged to move. The exertion caused his leg muscles to swell until he wondered if the neoprene suit would split. Then his back slid an inch up the tanks. He relaxed and heaved again, gaining two more inches. With the next heave the tanks slid away from behind him and he was able to straighten.

Now he had Lao's full weight by the hips. He slowly slid back down the wall. Now Lao sat straddling his upper legs. Most of the water was flowing over Lyons's knees. In this position he was able to keep their faces clear. He steadied Lao with his left hand at her neck and slid off her face mask with the right.

Gadgets had caught and was bracing the air tanks. Somehow he'd also managed to get his light on and shine it up the wall.

Lyons blasted the stale air out of his lungs and hungrily drew in a long breath from Lao's mouthpiece, then dropped the mask between them. Clamping her nose shut with his right hand, he covered her mouth with his, forcing her lungs full of air. Then he released her nose and snatched up the mask for more air. After his exertion, it took all his karate training to regulate his breathing in this fashion. It took nearly five minutes to make up his own oxygen deficit.

"How's it going?" Gadgets's voice hissed in Lyons's earplug receiver.

"Can't talk," Lyons managed to say between inhalations.

Suddenly Lao's tongue darted into Ironman's mouth, the first indication he received that she was regaining consciousness. Surprised, he jerked his head back.

Her chuckle was barely audible above the rushing water.

Lyons took the mouthpiece and drew a lungful of air, then passed the face mask to Lao. She drew air and passed the mask back.

"She's conscious," Lyons informed Gadgets.

"Good. These tanks are getting heavy."

"What happened?" Lao asked.

"An explosion. Knocked you out."

After her next breath Lao asked, "What caused the explosion?"

"Sulfides from decomposition, probably. We should know when we climb past the grate."

Before passing him the face mask, Lao tried some mouth-to-mouth resuscitation of her own to revive Lyons from his sense of lassitude.

"Be prepared to boost my tanks to me," Lyons told Gadgets. He took a last, long drag from the respirator.

Lao was still straddling him. Just before she slipped her mask back on, she leaned forward, her body pressed against his. "Now I know why you're called Ironman," she whispered. She braced her hands on his shoulders and worked her feet up until she stood on his knees. A second later she was climbing again.

Evidently Lao's comment had been picked up by her throat mike, as Gadgets asked, "What's happening up there?" with a touch of suspicion in his voice.

"Just switch the hoses, then boost the tanks," Lyons answered.

"Huh?"

"Lao's been doing all the heavy work. Then we both used her air supply. Switch hoses fast."

"Switching...*now*," Gadgets said to warn Lao about the temporary cut in air supply. Half a minute later he announced, "Your air's back, Lao. Here're your tanks, *Ironman*." There was some good-humored teasing in the emphasis on Lyons's nickname.

The tanks slid up the side of the tunnel. Leaning against them, Lyons adjusted them into place and did up the buckles. He was relieved to straighten his legs once more.

Lao's light shone on him from above and her voice came over the communicator, "Don't snag on the ends of the grating bars. The rope's tied off. I'll stand by to help."

The light above went off. Lyons shone his own light upward but a few feet beyond the bar ends saw only blackness. He climbed hand over hand to the grate. Lao's light reappeared to show him the jagged and bent ends. There was no way he and the tanks would fit through the opening.

"Pass up the tanks," Lao told him. She reached down and tied the rope to the tanks.

When Lyons felt the rope ease the weight of the tanks he undid the buckles. Lao hoisted the tanks through the opening. Lyons guided them with one hand, hanging from the rope with the other. When the tanks were clear, he boosted himself through the opening and stood with his feet on the ends of the cutaway steel bars, with nothing to brace his hands against. Lao steadied him as he clambered up four feet to stand on the floor of a large cave.

"Your turn, Hermann."

Lyons held the rope while Gadgets climbed through the jagged grating ends. Then he lifted Gadgets the last few feet into the cave.

Their lights on, they looked around. The huge cave had swallowed the light when they were below the grating, but now their flashlights illuminated two walls and the ceiling of the cave, though the far end remained dark. Water ran along a trench in the floor.

Now the cause of the explosion was evident. Whenever there was heavy use of toilets and garbage disposal units in the complex, the water overflowed its banks and deposited much of the waste on the nearly flat cave floor. The wet waste produced combustible gasses.

Gadgets whistled, a weird sound over a throat mike with a respirator going.

"You called the shot right again, Ironman."

"Careful. The floor's slimy," Lao warned them.

It was a relief to be able to walk, even on a slippery surface. They followed the channel for two hundred yards before reaching the continuation of the thirty-inch tunnel. Standing, they chewed on some high-energy bars and sipped Gatorade.

When they were finished, Lao stuck her head in the channel and said, "This is easier. We stay roped together and just climb."

It was easier. The tunnel now slanted at a thirty-degree angle instead of a sixty-degree angle. It was like climbing up a slippery, shallow roof.

Twenty minutes later Lao's voice came over the communicator. "End of the line," she said. "At this point our sewer breaks into three small ones. All too small to get through."

17

Blancanales asked the five members of SIGNET if any of them had handled rifles before.

"We're country hicks," Val reminded him. "All of us have."

Blancanales handed each one a Kalashnikov with a full clip and showed them where the safety was. He told them, "I've put these rifles on single shot—a bullet each time you squeeze the trigger. They're loaded and cocked. Don't forget to keep your line of fire away from the rest of us."

Knight helped position Manny, Zorro, Glitch and U.U. on the floor, two on each side of the door, where their cross fire would discourage terrorists in the hall. Blancanales had already thrown mattresses around the door for them to lie behind.

"Why can't we use automatic," asked Val, the last to receive a weapon.

"Not much ammunition. If you're not used to it, you won't hit anything. I want to keep the use of these Kalashnikovs close to the rifles you're familiar with," Blancanales told him.

"I've shot automatic weapons. My dad's Army. Said we should be able to defend ourselves."

"Wise man. Okay. Here's the fire selector. Keep the bursts small. Feel free to help Knight and I if necessary, but stay low."

Val started to turn away.

"Put two extra clips in your belt," Blancanales told him.

Knight examined the captured weapons. There were eight Kalashnikovs, a pile of spare clips and three Makarovs left.

"Do we split these?"

Blancanales shook his head. "I have all the ammunition I need for this." He patted his M-16/M-203 combo. "The rest of you keep those Russian weapons going as long as possible. We can't battle out of here. We simply have to hold out as long as we can."

Knight lowered his voice. "They can always burn us out."

"I know. But this is still a safer bet than open country. If fire starts we'll have to make a break."

"Fat chance."

Blancanales shrugged. He felt old and tired. He knew the youngsters' lives would probably be forfeited. He'd deliberately made the decision and it weighed heavily on his conscience. He could have evacuated the hackers immediately, but without the delaying tactics with the computer, Able Team would have had little chance of stopping the terrorists before they achieved their goal at the missile site.

Seven lives were being desperately gambled to save thousands. It made sense, but that didn't help his conscience one whit.

"DAMN TUNNEL CAN'T END HERE," Ironman said. "They didn't drill it from the other end."

After a pause Lao said, "Concrete cap, connected to the plumbing. One outlet is clean flow from the artesian wells. The other two spurt now and then—sewer pipes."

"We blast," Lyons decided.

"Great!" Gadgets groaned. "We all slide out of this damn water trough. I crawl up again and set the charges. I enjoy the slideway once more. We set off the blast and hope the cave doesn't fall on us. Then we fight our way through the rubble-strewn sewer once more. We get to the top. All the terrorists are staring at the ruined crappers. We yell, 'Surprise'! I love the idea.''

"What else?'' Lyons asked.

"What do you see?'' Gadgets asked Lao.

Lao made a thorough examination before reporting, "Ironman's right. It's a precast lid. Probably held in place by weight plus all the plumbing connected to it. I see where it fits into a lip on the tunnel.''

"What size are those pipes?'' Gadgets asked.

"The main one is about half the diameter of the one we're in. The other two are about six inches.''

"What are they made of?''

Several seconds later Lao answered, "Everything is so cold and slimy I had to scrape with my knife to make sure. It's that black plastic stuff.''

"PVC pipe,'' Gadgets said. "We're laughing. If we all unhook our tanks and masks, we should be able to play musical air lines.''

"What are you thinking?'' Lyons asked.

"If I set the charges, I can demolish the pipe without us having to leave the tunnel. Then, if you're top man when the blast goes off and we have pitons in place, you can do your Samson act. We'll have a fighting chance of getting out of here before we have to start shooting.''

"If we're not dead in the blast,'' Lao added.

"We're about out of air. We try it,'' Lyons decided.

They slid back a few feet and waited while Lao set the steel spikes into the sides of the tunnel. The pitons would allow Gadgets to work in a slight crouch. When Lyons was at the top of the shaft, his legs would be further bent so he could put his shoulders against the cement and thrust with his powerful leg muscles.

"Done,'' she reported.

"Attach two ends of the rope. We want to hang farther down the tunnel,'' Gadgets told her.

When she was finished, Lyons and Gadgets shrugged off their tanks and tied the harness to the ropes. Lao left her mask hanging on a piton and slid down to Lyons. He handed her sack of weapons to her before she continued her slide to Gadgets. Clambering over him, she made a loop in the rope for one foot. Using only that much support, she accepted his scuba gear and strapped it on.

Gadget climbed over Ironman and his double tanks to take his position under the cement lid. Ironman didn't put the tanks back on. He merely slid down until he could put on the face mask once more.

Gadgets put on Lao's face mask. Then he fished the demolition plastique out of his bag along with three radio-activated detonators. Reaching as far into each pipe as he could, he smeared on the plastique, then placed more a foot closer. The pipe was slippery and he had to scrape and work to make the plastique stick. He joined the two circles of plastique with another line of explosive and put a detonator halfway between them. Repeating the procedure for each of the three pipes took him half an hour.

"My air's gone," Lyons reported.

"Time to discard the scuba gear," Gadgets answered.

They undid the heavy bottles and let them slide to the cave. The air in the tunnel was foul, but didn't seem to be choking them. The gas generated in the cave was too heavy to rise up the tunnel and no waste had accumulated on the slope.

The three warriors slid down twenty feet from the end of the tunnel. Lyons took Gadgets's place at the head of the line. Then they each tied themselves to the rope.

"Three, two, one..." Gadgets droned.

All three covered their ears as Gadgets thumbed the detonator box.

It sounded like three, large-caliber rifles being fired side by side. A wave of explosive-driven water tried to wash them away. Then it was over.

Lyons scrambled up the rope, using it to find the pitons for his feet. Water no longer flowed from the openings, but the air, heavy with oxidation products, was unbreathable. He could hear cries of alarm from the complex above. Lyons put his shoulders against the cement cam and pushed. Nothing happened.

Lyons inhaled the foul air deeply and let half out. Then he let the other half out in an explosive shout. At the same time he snapped his leg muscles straight. The use of his karate breathing and those iron muscles blasted the lid free. It dropped two feet to the stone floor of a small, dark room.

Lyons flexed his legs again and straightened them with another snap, propelling himself into the room beyond the lid.

Lyons's flashlight showed a small service room. The shouting outside the room was getting closer.

Gadgets had placed the plastique perfectly. A foot length was missing from all three drain pipes. Water from the largest pipe was pouring steadily onto the floor. That would be the flow from the artesian wells. The hundred-pound concrete cover lay unbroken on the floor by the tunnel opening.

Gadgets and Lao popped from the opening and ripped open the waterproof sacks holding their weapons.

"Help me with the lid," Lyons told Gadgets.

Gadgets helped him lift the lid back in place.

"Why the sudden urge for neatness?"

Lyons didn't bother explaining. He tied his waterproof sack over the largest opening. Without further questions, Gadgets and Lao closed off the other openings. Lyons found some old paint cans that jammed tightly over the two smaller pieces of broken pipe. A wastebasket went over his sack on the largest piece. The water pouring into the room could no longer escape through the tunnel Able Team had used. By that time the voices were right outside the door, following the trail of water.

The three Stony Man warriors killed the lamps.

The door was thrown open. Three terrorists in jeans and plaid shirts stood in the doorway, squinting into the darkness at the black neoprene-suited figures.

Gadgets's silenced Beretta made the introductions. The terrorists acknowledged the formality by bowing forward. As they crumpled to the wet floor, Lyons jerked each one inside the room. Lao closed the door again.

"We're on the bottom of three levels. Clear this level first. We'll work our way up," Lyons ordered.

Gadgets opened the door slightly and peered down the hall.

The sounds indicated heavy occupancy, but the hall was empty except for a six-foot dark man staring toward them, wearing slacks and a sport shirt that fit well enough to have been tailored for him. A bandolier of grenades and shotgun shells adorned one shoulder. He carried a sawed-off double-barrel.

"*¿Por demoro tonto?*" the man demanded.

This was the leader, Gadgets decided, wanting to know what took his men so long. If he could get him to relax, they might get out of the utility room without getting caught in a deadly cross fire.

Gadgets quickly rattled off a reply in Spanish. Then he said softly to Ironman, "Now or never."

"What you tell him?"

"Pipe burst. We're shutting off the water."

Lyons looked at the strong flow from the artesian wells. No one could shut that off. He grinned and led the way out the door, his Konzak questing prey like a bird dog's nose.

The tall Puerto Rican dived through a doorway just before Ironman's assault shotgun sent him its love. From out of range he bellowed out a series of commands in Spanish.

Lyons didn't need to understand Spanish to know the results of those commands. "Take the first room," he ordered.

Gadgets and Lao ran for the nearest doorway as Lyons's automatic shotgun ripped up the heads of two butchers who leaned out of doorways ahead of them. The rest of the enemy remained hidden.

Lao ran with her knees pumping high, rapidly overtaking Ironman. Being the smallest, fastest moving target, she would take the unknown room first.

Gadgets ran backward, spraying the hall behind him with enough short bursts from his Mac-10 to discourage the terrorists from that half of the hall. He was the last to leap through the doorway, and did so just as the hall filled with a hail of lead from both directions. Smoke was billowing into the room, but there was not enough to cut visibility. Gadgets saw six Kalashnikovs seeking targets. Shooting back would be difficult. Bound prisoners were leaning against two walls.

IGNACIO QUADRA WAS FUMING. First the Russian idiots had fouled up the computer access. Despite Rivera's reassuring talk, Quadra was convinced they were up to something.

So he had to stretch the occupation of the missile site four hours while Rivera looked for computer help. Quadra was aware that his orders to execute the prisoners might not have been followed. Who was in charge, anyway? He'd have to make an example of someone. He hoped it wasn't his old friend Rivera.

And what was the Army doing up there? They'd tried only once to get through to him. He wasn't ready to talk to them yet, but why weren't they more anxious? What were they doing? Quadra glanced at his watch. Rivera would be at the abandoned CIA camp by now. How long would it take him to get back?

The terrorist leader's nervous thoughts were interrupted by a muffled explosion down the hall. Quadra grabbed his Kalashnikov and moved to the doorway of the room he was using for an office. He was too well trained to stick his head out and start shouting questions. He stood and listened.

Hearing only Spanish, Quadra stepped into the hall. To his left, he could see water pouring from under a closed door.

He watched three of his soldiers wade the new Amazon to determine its source. They opened the door, started to bend to look at the floor, then vanished inside, as if they had tripped. Why had the last one in closed the door again? Quadra shifted his feet, expressing his unease. The water continued to spread down the hall.

After much too long a time someone emerged. Quadra demanded to know what was taking them so long. The answer, in smooth Spanish, almost assuaged his fears. It took him several seconds to decide that no burst pipe would ever make a noise like the explosion he'd heard.

Quadra had many of the qualities needed for good leadership. One was the ability to make quick decisions. Once he decided he wasn't hearing the truth he exploded into action. A split second before a shotgun sent its deadly pellet storm down the hall, he dived back into the room he'd taken over for his temporary command post.

As soon as his hide was safe, he bellowed commands that could be heard through the level. He told his men to concentrate on eliminating the invaders. Only then did he start to wonder how the hell they could have gotten into the complex.

Glancing into the hall, he saw three forms dive into the room where the scientists and technicians were being held.

If the six guards didn't eliminate the intruders, a few grenades tossed into the room would. He shouted a command for his men to close in on the room and rose to join them.

Quadra kept his eye on the open door from which water still spread. No more fighters emerged. Perhaps these three had evaded his first search and managed to arm themselves.

Kalashnikovs burst into furious activity in the room where the three Don Quixotes had tried to hide. Quadra smiled as he signaled his men to cover the doorway.

TWO HOURS HAD PASSED since someone had casually tossed a grenade into the souvenir shop. Verna Odger had managed to wrap her arms around the surviving child and roll behind the counter. Later, staying well back from the large windows, she had watched the Army arrive and set up a perimeter about a quarter mile from the building. She decided there were other hostages, which would account for the Army's failure to move in and the criminals' not returning to finish their killing.

Weighing the situation carefully, she decided it would be safer to stay where she was than risk crossing open territory or calling attention to herself. So the white-haired woman settled in a chair near which she had stashed three loaded Uzis. Then she rocked the hysterical little girl as the child sobbed and finally dozed off from exhaustion.

Verna stayed alert. If the killers returned, she would not "go gentle into that good night," as Dylan Thomas had put it. She sat, rocking back and forth, holding the child. But her mind was not gentle. She was amazed at the depth and intensity of her rage.

18

Rivera, leading nine Puerto Ricans and eight Russian "specialists," expected no difficulty scooping up whichever hackers Fred White had kept alive for his own amusement. Besides, a dozen Free PR men still guarded the abandoned CIA site.

When the terrorists stopped their old school bus within sight of the barracks, no one came out to check on them. Alarm bells rang in Rivera's brain. He jumped to the door of the bus and ordered full battle alert.

A quick check of the site revealed the dead terrorists who had been killed outside the barracks. Rivera divided his troop into three six-man units. One unit surrounded the building to act as containment. Six men went in at each end of the hallway, which ran the length of the building.

They entered quietly and were greeted by silence. The huge piles of junk barricading access to the room where the hackers had been working suggested that someone was still holed up in there. It would be a simple matter to burn them out, but they needed the hackers alive, if possible.

No sounds issued from the workroom.

"Anybody here?" Rivera called.

He was answered by silence.

He thought about his situation and decided it was good. Whoever had filled the hall full of junk didn't know what he was doing. The stuff afforded perfect cover for closing in on the doorway. If the hackers had weapons, they had denied themselves clear fields of fire.

The Russian-trained terrorist rose and waved for the other group down the hall to start moving in. Already a Russian "specialist" from Rivera's group had crawled ten feet into the obstacle course. Rivera could see two more of the Russian kill specialists making good time on the other side of the junk heap.

The Russian was ten feet into the mound of old furniture when he encountered three strands of barbed wire stretched from behind a torn sofa against one wall to a chair against the opposite wall. He seized the wires and yanked them out of the way. Two grenades came with the wires, leaving pins and spoons behind.

"Down!" Rivera roared.

He leapt into the midst of his group, bowling them down like tenpins and falling across the heap.

The Russian who had unveiled the two surprise packages struggled to get away from them, but found himself in a situation where the junk left him little room for quick retreat. The double blast tore him to shreds.

A second later, another blast rocked the hall from the other side of the refuse heap. A Russian wailed a stream of agonized curses. Someone else screamed unrelentingly until his voice disappeared in a frothy gargle.

Rivera's group struggled to their feet. Their weak smiles showed how happy they were to have a leader who was large enough to bowl them all off their feet. Suddenly the hall no longer seemed the best way to sneak up on the hackers. There was a strong reluctance to lead the way into the mass of broken furniture, desks, chairs, garbage cans, bunk frames and a hundred other things.

Rivera sighed. He stood up and pulled a chair out of the way and handed it back for someone else to carry away. One at a time, he carefully disentangled each item and had it removed. It would take half an hour to reach the hackers, but he knew this was the only way he'd get the terrorists to follow him. It went against their beliefs to experience terror rather than distribute it.

WHEN THE BLASTS SHOOK THE HALL, Blancanales watched the young people closely, trying to determine how they were taking it. Their faces were pale. Glitch and Elvy bit their lips. But none of them suffered lack of nerve. Each stuck to his assigned post and stayed alert.

Val Tredgett sighted his Kalashnikov through one of the holes Blancanales had cut through the boards over the windows. He fired a short burst. Blancanales dashed across the room and pulled him down from the window just as a blast of 7.76 slugs cut through the hoarding.

"But I got him," Val exclaimed. "He was one of the assholes who kept us locked up here."

"Good," Blancanales answered. "But next time remember those boards won't stop bullets."

Val nodded. Reaction was setting in and he was fighting to hold himself together.

The questing fire from outside sliced across the other windows. Everyone was low and it did no damage. Blancanales got up and risked a quick look through a firing slot.

"They're keeping their distance," he reported.

"They know we're here now," Knight pointed out.

Blancanales said nothing. That could be assumed from the booby traps in the hall. He could hear the terrorists on one side of the hall still working to demolish his barricade. They'd be charging any minute now.

"I guess we can congratulate ourselves," Zorro said. His voice was hoarse from controlled nervousness.

"What about?" Knight asked.

"They're not burning us out. That means we won at Vault Invaders. Now they need us to untangle the computer again."

Knight wasn't as quick as the younger computer types, but he figured it out when they started the ball rolling. "You're basing your whole assumption on the fact that they haven't started a fire yet?" he asked Elvy.

"You got it."

Knight risked a quick look through a perforated hoarding before answering, "Don't forget we'll reach a point where we're just not worth the trouble."

Val looked through another hoarding, then ducked. When he was safely down he said, "Thought of that. What do we do then?"

His question was punctuated by a single shot from U.U.'s assault rifle.

"Missed," she reported.

Her shot and voice brought a hail of fire from both sides of the hall. Bullets chewed up the doorway.

"They're shooting high," Olga observed calmly.

"That won't keep up when they get really pissed off," Manny told her.

Blancanales shook his head. The kids were as calm as seasoned warriors. He should have realized that it took a particular type of unflappability to crack computer systems. If they could be prevented from doing malicious damage, society needed young people like this. Blancanales found a fierce, protective fire burning in his gut. He shook it off, knowing that these kids had a better chance of survival if they acted aggressively.

Zorro drew the next blood. He sighted and squeezed the trigger. The shot was followed by a Spanish curse from the hall.

"Just creased an arm," Elvy said to no one in particular.

"We're doing okay," Knight said encouragingly.

"Too well," Val answered. "I smell smoke."

ABLE TEAM PLUNGED from the frying pan of the hall into the heavy cross fire in a large room. Prisoners lined two sides of the room. They sat on the floor, propped against the walls. Each had his hands and feet bound in front of him and wore a blindfold. Most wore white lab coats.

Six terrorists guarded the prisoners. When the firing broke out in the hall, they turned toward the door, Kalashnikovs ready.

Lao was first through the door. She threw herself to the floor and rolled into the room. A splatter of lead hit the tile near her head. The bullets ricocheted and whined into the wall at shoulder height.

By the time the terrorists had figured they were in danger of shooting one another, Lyons was inside the door. His Konzak stuttered on full automatic, filling the room with 360 deadly pieces of lead shot, all flying at shoulder height.

Gadgets was through the door on Ironman's heels. Angry lead snapped behind the infiltration specialist. Gadgets's Mac-10 fired a short burst. All the .45s found their target, but three burst right through to buzz around the room like demented hornets.

Lao, lying on her back, took out the last terrorist to remain standing. The smaller 9 mm manglers from her Mac-11, traveling on an upward course, stayed inside the jackal's body. The neatness made no difference to the corpse.

Lao and Gadgets cut the prisoners free while Lyons watched the door. The scientists were pale and shaking, but none was injured. Only one succumbed to his fear. He wiped at the sticky stuff on his face. When his hand came away covered with gore, the scientist quietly fainted. The others struggled to their feet to get their heads out of the smoke that still drifted in from the hall.

Lyons barked at the rest of the prisoners, "Grab those weapons. You'll defend yourselves."

"We're no soldiers," a woman protested.

"Then you're dead," Lyons told her.

"What are we supposed to do?" someone else asked.

"Cover the hall from two sides of the doorway. If you see a terrorist, shoot. If they get back in here, you're dead."

"That's your job," the woman said.

Lyons ignored her. "Take your silencers off," he told Lao and Gadgets. "I want them to hear what we're doing."

The water from the hall reached the doorway and began to spread into the room.

"What's that?" someone asked.

"Just water and the contents of a bunch of glass containers," Lyons lied.

"Bacteria," someone whispered.

The scientists edged away from the water. Lyons looked at them, his disgust evident.

"It's our job to do our killing close up. You just kill at a distance. The water's not contaminated—yet. Save yourselves or die crying. I don't give a damn."

He pulled the pins from four smoke grenades and tossed two each way into the hall. Then Gadgets and Lao each tossed a wire-wound grenade into the hall, bouncing them off the walls toward opposite ends of the hall.

Lyons picked up a Kalashnikov, extended it arm's length into the hall and fired until the clip was empty. An answering yammer of autofire came from both ends of the hall. Able Team waited until most of the terrorists had exhausted their clips, then charged into the hall toward the next room.

The Konzak bucked and roared, making it impossible for anyone ahead of them to stick a head through a doorway to fire down the hall. Lao expended the remainder of her clip toward the other end of the hall. Between Lyons and Lao,

Gadgets ran through the water, touching the wall so they wouldn't pass the next door in the dense smoke.

"Here," Gadgets gasped when he found a doorframe.

The three warriors sprang into the room—an office, empty—just as the hall once again filled with 7.62 mm Russian goodwill.

Gadgets glanced at the desk. "Looks as if they used this for command headquarters until a few seconds ago," he remarked.

Lyons and Lao watched the door.

"Computer room's next. They'll have their firepower bunched at that point," Lyons said.

Before he could go on, there was the sound of autofire and then of rifle stocks hitting flesh. A woman screamed. The scream was cut off by a blow. Then a voice shouted Spanish through the thinning smoke.

Ironman looked to Gadgets for a translation.

"They recaptured the scientists," Gadgets told Lao and Lyons.

On the heels of Gadgets's translation, the terrorist leader supplied his own. His voice shouted from the direction of the computer room, "Hear that, you imperialist dogs? We have the scientists once more. Surrender or we'll execute the lot of them for crimes against humanity."

19

Quadra shouted at them from farther up the hall. The scientists had been recaptured in the room Able Team had just left. Lyons reached an instant decision and whispered his orders.

"You two retake the prisoners. I'll furnish the diversion."

There was no time for argument. Trusting Lyons's tactical sense, Lao and Gadgets freshened their weapons and waited.

Lyons slammed a 30-round magazine into the Konzak, then tossed a wire-wound grenade in either direction down the hall. The moment the double concussion shook them Ironman was out the door. He charged the computer room, his Konzak roaring its defiance.

Gadgets returned his cocked Ingram to its leg clip and pulled the silenced Beretta 93-R from shoulder leather. He extended the front grip, grabbing it with his left hand. Then he and Lao returned to the room they'd just left. They squinted through the thick smoke and held their weapons ready, but did nothing to announce themselves.

A terrorist popped out of the doorway, intending to send a spray of lead toward the disturbance. Instead the Beretta cleared its throat with a small cough and a subsonic parabellum poked him in the left eye, then proceeded into his brain. The creep didn't feel a thing. Lao reached the body before it fell and yanked it toward her.

A voice shouted in Spanish from the other side of the doorway, "José, you coconut head, come back."

Gadgets answered, *"Sí,"* and stepped almost up to the entrance. He could see most of the room, and those inside, he knew, could see a figure in the rapidly thinning smoke.

As they squinted to see what was happening, Gadgets's Beretta spoke. Knees bent, using a two-hand firing stance, the infiltration specialist lined up on the Free PR goons while the 93-R dealt with them one at a time.

Three Puerto Rican terrorists collapsed before realizing that it wasn't José in the hall. Their eyes were so focused on the figure in combat crouch they failed to notice the smaller figure who was on her stomach and had crawled around the doorway.

Gadgets stepped to one side of the opening just as the remaining three terrorists managed to react. Their bullets screamed through the door at waist height and above. Below the stream of deadly lead, Lao calmly sent three bursts of 9 mm death from her Mac-11. The last three terrorists crumpled to join the other corpses littered around the floor.

Gadgets slapped a new magazine into the Beretta and exchanged it for his own Ingram. He went farther down the hall to make sure they had the last of the terrorists. By this point he was splashing through more than an inch of water.

Lao stepped into the room and said coldly, "You were told to protect yourselves." She changed clips as she spoke.

The same woman who'd tried to give Lyons a hard time spoke up again. "That's not our job. You must assign men to protect us."

Lao didn't waste time arguing. She stepped over to the woman and delivered a slap that sent her reeling across the room. "The next time you open your mouth, I'll shoot you for treason," Lao told the woman.

Then she stepped into the hall, which was remarkably free from flying lead. Down the hall, the boom of Ironman's Konzak was being met by the steady rattle of Kalashnikovs.

Gadgets appeared out of the thinning smoke. "No more survivors that way."

Lao and Gadgets both started to run for the computer room side by side, weapons questing the hall ahead.

LYONS'S CHARGE UP THE HALL was not as suicidal as it seemed. The steady roar of the assault shotgun discouraged anyone from sticking his head out to fire back. Someone tried pitching out a grenade, only to have it blasted out of his hand to explode in the doorway. The blast was too far from Lyons for the small bits of wire to reach him.

Plucking a grenade from his belt, Lyons pulled the pin with his teeth. His right hand squeezed the trigger of his Konzak sporadically to discourage terrorists farther up the hall from launching a counteroffensive. The big weapon bucked too heavily for accurate one-hand use, but Lyons had no specific target.

The heavy steel door to the computer room was closed. Those inside had also considered the possibility of grenades being tossed into the room. Lyons strode past the closed door and disposed of his grenade by bouncing it off the open door to the next room in line. The blast propelled a Kalashnikov into the hall.

Lyons stepped quickly into the room, but its only occupant was a grenade-splattered corpse. The man had been crouching near the open door, waiting to pop out when Lyons stopped to change magazines.

"All things come to he who waits," Lyons told the shredded corpse.

He checked out the last two rooms in the hall. Empty. Beyond them was the ramp to the next level. Ironman stayed clear of that. He returned to meet Gadgets and Lao by the closed steel door.

"C-4," Ironman ordered.

Gadgets packed the plastic explosive into the small cracks around the door. Lyons stood directly behind him, Konzak ready. If anyone opened the door suddenly he was in for a faceful of lead. Lao kept a wary eye on the corridor. Two inches of water cooled their feet.

Two minutes later Gadgets nodded and they retreated to the next room. Lyons changed clips, putting in six rounds of micro-grenades. As soon as Gadgets trigged the small blast, the three warriors charged back into the corridor. The steel door and its jamb had been blasted out of the rock wall to fall just inside the room. Two terrorists lay broken under the ton weight of the door.

"My okruzheny," someone shouted from inside.

"Da! Da! My okruzheny," another voice chanted.

Lyons cocked an eyebrow at Lao. "Russian?"

"Yes. They surrender."

"Prisoners worth questioning. Let's take them."

Lyons leapt inside the door, Konzak ready. Inside were three older men wearing North American business suits, with their hands in the air. Three younger men, similarly attired, lay dead on the floor. The two terrorists left to guard the Russians had died when the door fell on them. The cause of death of the younger Russians was more puzzling.

Lyons used his boot to turn one corpse onto its stomach. The back of his head had been smashed.

"Komitet Gosudarstvennoi Bezopasnosti," one prisoner explained.

Lyons didn't need a translator to recognize the name of the KGB. The fanatical Russian secret police would have insisted that the scientists fight to the death. Beyond doubt the KGB would have killed the scientists rather than have them alive to answer American questions. The scientists had solved their no-win dilemma simply and directly.

Each member of Able Team snapped plastic cuffs on a prisoner. Lyons waved to communicate that they should follow, but stay well back. The three scientists exchanged dubious glances but did as indicated.

Lyons removed the unused grenades and snapped a clip of special loads containing steel shot into the Konzak. When everyone was in the hall, he turned back and opened up in full auto. The assault shotgun roared and kicked. When it was finished, two $600,000 computers were ready for a scrap dealer.

"Just in case they're stalling," he told Lao.

The six of them waded through three inches of water to the foot of the ramp. Lights flickered and went out. Emergency, battery-powered lamps came on at each end of the ramp.

"Water's reached the electrical circuits," Gadgets observed.

He raised his silenced Beretta and put out the battery-operated lights. In the bare stone tunnel between floors the silenced gun didn't threaten to burst their eardrums.

They trudged up the ramp in the dark. The Russians followed hesitantly. It was a relief to stop splashing through water. Their boots squished noisily, but no one fired down on them. At the top of the ramp they reached a closed door.

"Why didn't they have a couple of rifles at the top to slow us down?" Gadgets wondered.

It was pitch-dark, but he could visualize Ironman's shrug. Gadgets didn't need to warn his teammates the door might be booby-trapped. None of them had made a hasty grab for the handle.

Gadgets pushed people back and wrapped some tape around the knob. He crouched and pulled on the tape. The knob turned, but nothing else happened. He stayed crouched and unwound more tape, keeping the tension on the door handle. The door swung open. No blast. No gunfire. He carefully rewound the tape and stored it away again before approaching the open door. The hall of the second level was deserted except for two bodies no one had bothered to move.

The second level was illuminated by the dim light shed by emergency lights. This time Gadgets didn't bother to extinguish them before advancing. They checked each room as they came to it. The area was quiet as a tomb. It was a tomb in which the bodies of American defenders were scattered.

The floor was given over to storerooms and to laboratories in which germ cultures were grown. Each lab showed signs of having been hastily looted. Able Team reached the ramp to the top level without encountering anyone. The silence and the semidarkness were eerie.

Gadgets carefully put the tape over the handle of the door to the ramp leading to the top level of the cave complex. This time he crouched farther to one side before he pulled the tape to twist the handle. The Russians looked at him as if he were only slightly demented. The latch clicked and the door began to swing open. Then it was blasted across the corridor to smash on the opposite wall.

While the others were trying to shake the ringing out of their ears, Lyons leapt over the rubble and fired six fast loads of buck up the ramp.

Then the members of Able Team charged up the ramp, forgetting the ringing in their ears. Lyons's shotgun was as hard on them as the blast had been. Ironman changed clips on the run. The Russians followed at a fast walk, glancing around fearfully.

The three warriors reached the top of the ramp just as the terrorists reacted to the assault with a rush from the other direction. Two Ingrams and the Konzak exploded into action half a second before the goons could bring their Russian-supplied weapons into line. It rained pieces of scum halfway down the corridor.

Then Quadra stepped into the middle of the hall with his arms stretched straight to either side. In each hand was a flask of pink liquid.

"Go ahead and shoot, imperialist dogs," the terrorist leader shouted. "When one of these flasks breaks, the plague is released."

As THE SMOKE wafted down the hall of the old barracks building, the terrorists fired at the hoarded windows and down the hall toward the door. The message was loud and clear, "No way out!"

"Quick," Blancanales ordered. "Drag the mattresses to that side of the room and get behind them."

Blancanales watched the door while his orders were obeyed. Moving all the junk into the hall had taken more of his energy than he cared to admit. He kept one hand on the doorpost to prevent himself from waving like a blade of grass in the wind.

The buzzards kept up the occasional volley down the hall and made no attempt to charge. Blancanales decided to risk ignoring them for thirty seconds. He shuffled over to the pile of mattresses and knelt behind them.

"Everyone over here," he commanded.

When they were crouched behind the barrier, Blancanales laid three HE grenades against the far wall. Then he hurried across the room, knelt at the opening and used three more to blast the far wall of the next room. Signaling for the rest to follow, he staggered to the next opening and used the last of his HEs to breach a third wall.

Blancanales caught his breath while Knight taped two grenades against the window. When the grenades were ready, Blancanales shuffled to the door and used the M-203 to send two phosphorus grenades exploding over the heads of the nearest terrorists.

Screams shook the building as the fragments of burning metal penetrated human bodies and continued to burn. The smudges that were being used to force the defenders into a retreat were replaced by raging flames.

Knight let the spoons fly from the two grenades, sprinted across the room and dived through the hole in the wall. After the blast, he and the five hackers ran to the damaged hoards and knocked them away from the window with rifle butts.

One at a time they dived out the window and rolled into prone firing position. By the time the perimeter guards reacted to the appearance of their prey four rooms away there was a base of firepower outside the window. Blancanales, the last one from the building, took his time climbing out. The others sprang to their feet, anxious to beat the terrorists to their own bus.

Blancanales staggered. His combo gun was plucked from his exhausted fingers. Val carried the weapon. Ursula draped his arm over her shoulders. The group made slow time toward their objective.

Two more psychopaths rounded the edge of the building, to be cut down by three Kalashnikovs taken from the dead comrades-in-gore. Manny calmly picked up the fallen weapons and two spare clips and rejoined the group.

When they reached the end of the barracks, Knight and Val knelt with rifles facing the door of the building while the rest loaded onto the bus.

Blancanales tried to climb into the driver's seat but was easily steered away by Ursula. She sat him in a window seat and slid close to prop him up. Zorro started the bus, then went to sit near the door.

The sound of the bus engine jolted Rivera from his laborious furniture moving. He was checking each object for booby traps before moving it. No more traps were found, but no one was willing to bet his life there wouldn't be another one.

The surviving five terrorists dropped the junk they were moving, snatched up their Kalashnikovs and stumbled over the clutter of debris, rushing for the door. They burst out, oblivious of the two forms kneeling twenty-five feet away.

When all five were out, both Knight and Val Tredgett shot two lazy figure eights across the group. Then they dropped the empty weapons and ran for the bus. None of the terrorists felt like objecting. None could object.

"Where to?" Knight asked as he climbed into the driver's seat.

Blancanales haltingly told him how to find Seneca Rocks Recreation Area.

"Good," Val said. "I think we deserve an outing."

"Beer's on me," Blancanales told them.

He slipped into unconsciousness on Ursula's shoulder before the applause died down.

20

Lyons locked eyes with Ignacio Quadra, leader of an independence movement no one wanted.

The big terrorist grinned as he held the two culture flasks out from his sides.

"The plague, just for you."

The wide, white grin flashed again.

Lyons squeezed the trigger. The Konzak roared. The grin dissolved into a spray of flesh, teeth and bits of bone.

Before the flasks hit the floor, Lao's and Gadgets's Ingrams joined the chorus. Six more butchers succumbed to the meat grinder.

Able Team leapt the pink puddles on the tile floor, pursuing the remaining killers. The Russian scientists followed at a slower pace, gingerly stepping around the contaminated area.

The three warriors pressed the remaining terrorists, but were kept from closing by an almost steady stream of Russian-formed lead. The last eight of Quadra's goons made it to the ramp that led to the exit. The two elevators were waiting at the bottom. By keeping their Kalashnikovs trained on the ramp, the terrorists managed to keep Able Team at bay until the elevator doors closed.

"Watch the prisoners. Cover the elevators," Lyons snapped at Gadgets.

Gadgets positioned himself where he could fire into either elevator if it returned. The scientists wandered toward him. He motioned them to a safe corner.

One continued to approach, speaking Russian. When he saw that Gadgets didn't understand, he switched to labored, heavily accented English.

"Plis, fix germ water, I. I fix."

He had to repeat his request twice before Gadgets nodded. Gadgets pulled his Gerber. The Russian quailed, but Gadgets thrust the knife under one cuff and cut the wrist free. The scientist smiled his relief and held out the other wrist. Gadgets cut the cuff off that, too.

The stocky Russian ambled down the corridor, poking his head through every door he came to. When he reached a janitor's cupboard, he poked around in that, occasionally stepping back to examine something in the beam of an emergency light. Finally he emerged with a bottle of bleach, smelled it and nodded to himself.

He took the bottle and dumped the contents into the puddle formed by the flasks. Then he returned to the closet for a mop and used it to stir the two liquids around. Satisfied, he leaned the mop against the wall and walked back to Gadgets, presenting his wrists for a new set of cuffs.

As there were no indicators on the elevators, Gadgets was forced to keep his eyes on the elevator doors all the time. Without looking away, he handed the Russian his knife, indicating he should cut his companions free. The Russian was puzzled but did so, then returned the knife, which Gadgets slid back in its arm sheath.

The Russians seemed cooperative. If both elevators returned at once, there was a good chance Gadgets would go down because there was nothing for him to hide behind. He preferred the Russians have a chance to flee. The terrorists would kill them for surrendering.

Gadgets stared at the elevator doors, alert, tense, on edge.

DESPITE THEIR SUPERB CONDITIONING, Lao and Lyons really had no chance to beat the elevators to the top of a sixty-foot run.

The two martial artists paced themselves to keep from building too large an oxygen deficit. They didn't want to arrive at the top puffing too hard to shoot straight. The neoprene suits had bathed them in sweat. Lyons knew his temperature was rising because he couldn't dissipate body heat quickly enough, but he kept stretching his leg muscles and pushing.

Lyons's much longer legs slowly pulled him ahead of Lao's smooth two-stairs-at-a-time pace. Lyons pulled himself up three at a time.

At the top of the long climb Lyons cracked the heavy door open. No sound. He kicked it the rest of the way, Konzak ready. The elevators stood open. The sound of gunfire crackled from behind a steel security door leading to the shop in front of the building. Lyons ran five paces to the employee entrance and threw the door open.

"Anyone come out here?" he bellowed.

"Who's that?" someone shouted back.

"Santa Claus. Any terrorists come out this way?"

Ernest Cowley stepped into sight. "What's happening?" he demanded.

This time the rattle of gunfire was clearer. It was coming from the souvenir shop. It was accompanied by the screams of a child. Lyons turned and looked back. Lao had reached the top of the stairs and was covering the security door.

"Try that door," Lyons said. "I'll go around."

As he sprinted for the front of the souvenir shop, Lyons heard gunfire rattle again. Who was getting killed in there?

VERNA WAS STILL HOLDING the little girl cradled in her right arm when she heard the security door in the back of the souvenir store open. She snatched up an Uzi with her left hand and held it across her body, trained on the doorway that led to the small room in the back.

The doorway was suddenly filled with two goons holding Kalashnikovs at the ready. Verna swept a line of 9 mm parabellums across their chests before they could line up their weapons. The two terrorists staggered back into the arms of their brothers-in-blood.

The sudden burst of gunfire right by her ear awakened the frightened girl. At first she was too disoriented to react.

Still carrying the girl, Verna slid out of the chair and moved behind the counter. Several bursts of gunfire from the back room smashed shelving above their heads. The girl started to scream.

Verna kept the child between herself and the counter. She emptied the clip into the back room to discourage rash attacks, then snatched up a fresh weapon. The child continued to scream, a high, nerve-jangling expression of pure terror.

The terrorists were desperate to escape the apparitions in black neoprene who'd chased them from the bowels of the mountain. They heard the Uzi click empty and charged once more. The first one through the door had his head blasted into steak tartar. The other three decided not to charge just yet.

As they crouched, one produced a grenade. At that moment one of the devils in black neoprene charged through the front of the store. They were so overwhelmed by his sudden appearance that they failed to notice the door opening behind them. Suddenly the grenade was plucked from the terrorist's trembling hand. At the same time the barrel of a Mac-11 clipped another scum behind the ear.

Before they realized what was happening, the last three members of Free PR were prisoners.

Lyons saw that Lao had control of the terrorists. He snapped plastic cuffs on them while she kept them covered. Then he strode over to the woman and child.

Verna Odger's first words to Lyons were, "Young man, you'll pass out from heat exhaustion if you don't take that diving suit off."

Lyons suddenly realized his body was burning hot. He looked around in confusion.

"Don't worry about what you don't have on under it," Odger snapped. "I find it insulting that you'd imply I don't know what a male body looks like."

She turned to Lao. "You'd better do the same thing. And thank you. Both of you."

When E-4 came bursting into the souvenir shop followed by a dozen of his men, Verna Odger was sitting rocking a sobbing child. Lao and Lyons were lying flat on the floor, panting, clad only in light underpants.

"What the hell's happening?" Cowley demanded.

Without getting up, Lyons told him, "Three prisoners in the back room...three more at the base of the elevator. Russian scientists. One of my men with them. Some of your mad scientists survived. They're swimming around on the lowest level."

"Get dressed," Cowley ordered.

"Get our clothes from Hofstetter," Lyons snapped back.

Unable to get any more conversation out of the Stony Man warriors, Cowley had three of his men take away the prisoners. One was to return with the clothing. E-4 and the other nine went through the shop to the elevators and went down for the remaining prisoners.

GADGETS SAW BOTH SETS of elevator doors start to open at once. He crouched and brought the Mac-10 to bear. The first person to spill out was six-feet-four-inch Ernest Cowley in his three-piece suit. Gadgets jerked his weapon up. His hand had been so tense three bullets went into the ceiling from the suddenness of the movement.

Ten CIA hotshots dived for the floor, scrambling to bring their subguns into play without shooting one another. Gadgets straightened, grinning at the sight.

"Hello, E-4. Don't you know enough to knock before barging into a battle zone? What would dear old mater say if you had to take your ass home to get it sewn back on?"

The CIA types picked themselves up, exchanging looks of horror. These men would infiltrate enemy lines to spy and assassinate. They'd kill American citizens if so directed. Probably they'd take on the entire Russian army if the orders came. But none of them would have dared talk to Ernest Cowley IV in that flip tone.

"I'll have your balls for this," Cowley muttered as he brushed himself off.

Gadgets made a display of yawning. "If that's what turns you on. I was expecting enemies, but not your particular type."

"Where are the prisoners?"

Gadgets whistled. The three Russian scientists emerged from the corridor.

"What are they doing loose?" E-4 demanded.

"Coming when called. They're all yours."

Gadgets smiled and waved at the scientists as he stepped on the elevator and poked the Up button. He left Cowley still shouting something about proper procedure.

Gadgets reached the parking lot just in time to see a yellow school bus trundle up. The hackers jumped out, followed much more slowly by Blancanales. Knight stayed slumped at the wheel.

Gadgets ran to Blancanales, stunned by the tiredness in his face.

Lao and Lyons, wearing fatigues once more, emerged from the souvenir shop. They escorted a small, well-shaped lady of about sixty. The woman held a terrified but quiet child.

"Meet Verna Odger. She rounded up the last of the animals," Lyons said. He looked pleased.

The white-haired lady nodded. She seemed dazed by the attention.

Lyons turned to Blancanales. "You seem to have gotten them all through alive. The delay worked. Nothing was launched."

"Until next time," Blancanales said grimly.

Gadgets laughed. "No next time for this place. The bottom section's flooding now. I turned our captured scientists loose and they obligingly finished destroying anything we missed."

Lyons grinned. "E-4 will shit himself."

Gadgets assumed an air of injured innocence. "Can I help it if the terrorists were destructive? It's their nature."

The four comrades laughed.

Lyons turned back to Blancanales. "I've got orders for you."

Blancanales pulled his exhausted body together and waited.

"Take that magnificent nurse of yours and go on vacation. I don't want to see you for two months or until you're fit."

Blancanales grinned. "I'll try to bear up under your onerous commands."

"Whatever that means," Lyons said.

Blancanales took the child from Verna Odger and held her on his shoulder. Then he wrapped his free arm around Verna's shoulder and led the two of them away.

You don't know what
NONSTOP HIGH-VOLTAGE ACTION
is until you've read your
4 FREE GOLD EAGLE NOVELS

LIMITED-TIME OFFER

Mail to Gold Eagle Reader Service

In the U.S.
2504 West Southern Ave.
Tempe, AZ 85282

In Canada
P.O. Box 2800, Station A
5170 Yonge St.,
Willowdale, Ont. M2N 6J3

YEAH! Rush me 4 free Gold Eagle novels and my free mystery bonus. Then send me 6 brand-new novels every other month as they come off the presses. Bill me at the low price of $2.25 each— a 10% saving off the retail price. There are no shipping, handling or other hidden costs. There is no minimum number of books I must buy. I can always return a shipment and cancel at any time. Even if I never buy another book from Gold Eagle, the 4 free novels and the mystery bonus are mine to keep forever.

Name _____ (PLEASE PRINT)

Address _____ Apt. No. _____

City _____ State/Prov. _____ Zip/Postal Code _____

Signature (If under 18, parent or guardian must sign)

This offer is limited to one order per household and not valid to present subscribers. Price is subject to change.   166-BPM-BPGE

MYSTERY BONUS GIFT   HV-SUB-1